ANOTHER FIVE DAYS

A NOVEL

Matt Micros

For the best days that have yet to come...

ISBN-13: 9780996252652

<u>*Also by Matt Micros*</u>

~Five Days~

~Nick Nelson Was Here~

~The Music Box~

~Slow Drinkers, Giant Ballbags & Smelly Bastards~

~The Untold Tale of Shady Badesso~

TABLE OF CONTENTS

ANOTHER FIVE DAYS

For family and friends lost. I look forward to
our reunion whenever that may be…

This book is a work of fiction.
No part of the contents, even those depicting
real people, events, or conversations, actually
happened. It is a work of fantasy.

Chapter 1
Al Sokratis

Al Sokratis was a hero to everyone but himself. A Vietnam veteran, Blue Cross volunteer, school teacher, Mayor, husband, father and grandfather, he never did anything because he thought it would bring him good karma or fortune. He did it because that's what decent people did.

A few more rings around the oak tree had slowed him a bit, but he remained active in his late 70's, albeit a little bored. Every morning began the same way, and it didn't matter if it was snowing, raining, sunny or somewhere in between. He would walk the half mile into the Stonington Borough in the center of his sleepy Connecticut town, with his faithful Weimeraner companion, Hobbs, by his side, to buy copies of the *Daily News* and the *New London Day*, along with a coffee from the local convenience store. He lived in Connecticut, but followed all the New York sports teams, even though he lived closer to Boston than New York City. He liked the *Daily News* because he found the New York Times to be like watching Jeopardy when he was a Wheel of Fortune guy. The coffee wasn't particularly good; in fact, he could make a better cup at home, but it was tradition. Al would then walk home and sit on his front porch during nice weather and inside his sun room when it was lousy, reading the papers, pausing to occasionally wave to kids headed to the school bus stop.

He loved the smell and feel of a crisp newspaper before wrinkles and folds had taken place. Logging onto a computer to read the day's news didn't have the same feel to it, plus he wasn't a "surfer", internet or otherwise. It felt too much like using a calculator on the SAT.

Investigating the investigator. Disparaging nicknames from the President. A do-nothing Congress more interested in lining their own pockets than actually legislating. And a press that had become more editorial than an actual news reporting service. All of which left Al longing for the days of "Old Iron Pants" Walter Cronkite, when you didn't know how reporters personally felt about a situation because they never said. When he had enough of the negativity, he put down the paper and turned on SportsCenter. Surely that would be a welcome distraction he thought, until the first two stories were about athletes kneeling during the national anthem and refusing a celebratory visit to the White House. As a veteran, he found both to be disrespectful to the country and office. He shook his head and turned off the television just as the doorbell rang. No good news came at 7:30 in the morning he determined and he briefly contemplated whether it warranted grabbing his rifle, until he concluded that mass murderers usually didn't ring the bell.

He glanced sideways through his living room window and saw his grandson on the front porch. He was in his mid 20's, handsome like his father, an accountant for a financial investment firm, which seemed counter-intuitive to Al. Shouldn't finance firms be able to track their own money?

"Sammy? Is everything ok?" Al asked as he stepped aside to let him enter.

"Everything is better than ok. Everything is great!" was the response, before adding, "Did I wake you up?"

"I'm seventy-seven years old. I've been up since 5:00. And pretty much every hour on the hour before that."

"Good. So I've got some good news I wanted to share, along with a favor to ask and it couldn't wait."

Al nodded. "Ok. What's the good news?"

"I asked Delaney to marry me...and she said YES."

"That's terrific news. In fact, that's so terrific, it calls for a celebration," Al said as he pulled out two tumblers and a boxed bottle of scotch whiskey."

"A little early for whiskey, isn't it?" Sam questioned.

"If there was ever a time for Scotch at 7:30 in the morning, this is it. I've saved this bottle for just such an occasion. It's 30 year old Scotch Whiskey."

Al put a few cubes of ice into both glasses, unboxed the bottle and twisted it open with a decisive *crack* of the cap. He poured each glass about 1/3 full and handed one of them to Sam.

"Ya sou!" Al toasted, "and remember, it isn't a shot. It's to be sipped and enjoyed."

Sam took a small sip and winced as if someone had waterboarded him with turpentine. "If it tastes this bad after thirty years, I can't imagine how it tasted when it was first blended."

"Scotch is an acquired taste," Al smiled.

"Maybe acquired after your taste buds go bad when you get old?"

Al chuckled. "So what's the favor? Need some money for the wedding? Help planning the honeymoon?"

"Neither. I want you to be my best man."

"I'm flattered," was Al's measured response, "but you have hundreds of friends closer in age that would probably be better suited for that job."

"There is no one better suited for it than you. When my mom died and my dad ended up in jail, you and Gram took me in. And when she died, you continued to be there for me whether I needed advice, help financially, or just someone to talk to. My dad, for all of his warts, will always be my dad, but you're my best friend, and I want you to be my best man."

Tears welled up in the normally unflappable former Army gunner. "When you put it that way...how could I refuse?"

"You can't," Sam smiled.

"I'm honored. I'm truly honored. This is without a doubt the greatest honor I've ever received."

"Umm, you received a Purple Heart."

"That is a distant second to this."

As Sam hugged his grandfather tightly, Al couldn't help but think this had already become one of the greatest days of his life, and it was only a few hours old.

An hour later, Al drove along in his Ford F-150 pickup truck, playing the air trumpet with one hand to Glenn Miller's "In the Mood" as if he was the lead trumpet. It was a great day. Check that. An amazing day. The kind you had once every few years, where the skies were blue, the air crisp, and the lights all turned green when you approached.

Unfortunately, it didn't appear to be that way for everyone. Al came around the bend and immediately saw the smoke and flames of a car that was upside down on its roof with the wheels still spinning. There were people huddled around the car on the sidewalk, but no one was actually doing anything. A few people even pulled their phones out to video the scene. Al shook his head as he skidded to a stop partially blocking the road to protect the accident scene and hustled to the car as fast as a 77 year old could hustle. The man inside was still strapped into his seat, his face bleeding from the airbag. The window had shattered on impact.

"You ok?" Al asked, leaning in. "We've got to get you out of here. Your car is on fire and could blow at any minute."

"My legs are pinned against the dash and I can't reach the button to undo my belt," the man answered surprisingly calmly.

Al nodded as he pulled on the door, but it was dented and bent so it wouldn't pull open. He gave it another pull. Nothing. Of course no one else came over to help. But they were filming him. He then summoned every last ounce of energy in his body and he yanked the door open to the sound of creaking metal. He reached across the man and released the seat belt.   Grabbing him under his armpits, he pulled him from the vehicle and dragged him to the sidewalk to the applause of the idiots that had watched the entire thing.

"This car could blow! Everyone better get back!" Al bellowed before going back to move his own truck out of the way.

"Look out!" someone shouted.

Al looked up just in time to see a black Range Rover headed directly for him.

Chapter 2
Dennis Devine

Dennis Devine married his high school sweetheart a week after graduating from college. The younger versions of themselves were a perfect match. He was the Captain of the football and baseball teams, while she was the head cheerleader. They were both popular, smart and completely disinterested in politics. Neither envisioned a time where they wouldn't be a part of each other's lives, and yet they started their college days in different areas of the country. He went to Miami of Ohio in Oxford, Ohio, while Sheri stayed home and attended the University of Connecticut. After a year of late night phone calls with people screaming in the background, lonely dances, and hearing about friends that neither had met, he transferred back home. It was both the best and worst decision he ever made. The best because it saved their relationship. And the worst for the exact same reason.

By the time they married, they had become different people, but they were too comfortable and it was easier not to acknowledge that fact. Dinners were quiet as neither was interested in what the other had to say. She grew interested in politics, with a far left leaning bent. He thought all politicians were trash and he refused to waste a single breath on them. He loved all sports, but especially the Mets. She found baseball only slightly more exciting than what it would be like to watch grass grow in the desert.

They collectively thought that having a child might bring them closer together, but when it had the opposite effect, they decided to have a second. And then a third. The result was that they were drawn in three different directions, and became more roommates than husband and wife, waving as they passed each other in the driveway, two cars passing in the night.

***

Dennis was pulling his navy blazer on as he walked down the stairs into the kitchen. Sheri slid a glass of orange juice down the island counter to him and he grabbed a banana from the bowl in the middle.

"Can you drop off Jenny and Pete at the high school? They missed the bus," Sheri asked in a tone that was more of a demand than a question.

"Again?" he grumbled.

"Jenny took too long putting on her makeup for her boyfriend," Pete revealed.

"That's not true. I couldn't even get into the bathroom for an hour after Pete took a dump in there."

"Jenny! That is not how a lady talks!" Sheri exclaimed.

"And that's completely false," Pete responded.

"Mom and dad already called a fumigator. That's how bad it was."

"Enough with the potty talk. Whoever's coming with me, let's go. I have places to go and people to see," Dennis said as he ushered them out the door.

"Do you think you can both manage to not miss the bus home this afternoon?" Dennis asked as they strapped themselves into their seats. Jenny flew co-pilot while Pete sat in the back.

"Depends if Jenny can manage to stop making out with her boyfriend on time."

"Shut up, twerp."

"Don't make out with your boyfriend in public. That makes people uncomfortable," Dennis said diplomatically.

"Is that why you don't ever kiss mom in public?"

"That's exactly why."

"Fine. I'll do it in my bedroom then."

"You will absolutely *not* do it in your bedroom, young lady."

"His bedroom?"

"No one's bedroom!" Dennis exclaimed, veins bursting out of his forehead. "You don't want to develop a reputation."

"Too late for that," Pete said.

"Shut it, twerp. Not my fault no one wants to go out with you since you're such a geek."

"Jenny. That's not nice or true. Apologize to your brother."

"No, it's pretty much true," Pete nodded. "But it's ok. They'll love me someday when I'm bringing in seven figures and Jenny's boyfriend is pumping gas at the local Citgo."

Dennis couldn't help but chuckle at the response. "Have a good day, guys. I'll see you tonight."

Dennis had stopped at the same Starbuck's in nearby Mystic every morning before work for the past five years, partly because he was a man of routine and partly because he was infatuated with the girl behind the counter. She was in her late 20's and he knew unlikely to be interested in an old married guy with two kids, but there was definitely some type of banter and attraction that he couldn't explain.

"You're later than normal today," the girl behind the counter stated with a smile. She was tall and thin with green eyes as wide as saucers and long dirty blonde hair with plentiful curls that you couldn't really see when her hair was pulled back. Erika was the sort of woman that had underrated good looks. When in her work clothes, you'd nod and think she was cute, but dolled up for a night out and she had the capability of taking your breath away.

"I had to drop two of the kids off at the high school," Dennis answered.

"High school?! Did you get married when you were in 8th grade?" she smiled.

"Yes, we did. It was difficult at first to get someone to marry us, but eventually we found this nice Justice of the Peace who was also a witch doctor. I'm actually probably younger than you."

"I'm 28."

"Well, then we're the same age."

"You're funny," Erika laughed heartily.

"Tell that to my wife. She doesn't find me very funny. She used to, but not anymore."

"Maybe she needs a better sense of humor?"

"So what are you doing on this fine day?" he asked as she placed his mint hot chocolate with a dollop of whip cream down on the counter in front of him.

Erika took his card and rang him up. "After I get off at 1:00, I'm headed straight for the beach to try out my new bikini. You should see it. It's really cute. I'm wearing it underneath my uniform," she said, pulling back her collar to reveal a white string.

"A bikini can't be cute. It's the person that makes the bikini, not the other way around."

"You think?"

"Definitely."

"Thanks a lot. Now I'm going to be self-conscious," she frowned.

"I would definitely not be self-conscious if I were you. I'm sure you will look wonderful. Maybe I'll see you there. I'm actually wearing my American flag Speedo under my suit."

"Will the flag be half-staff or all the way up?" she winked.

"Umm....Umm."

The man next in line raised his eyebrows and smiled at the remark. He seemed to be enjoying the banter.

"I'm just teasin! Look at you blush!"

"I'm not blushing," Dennis answered while a crimson shade of red. "And it will definitely be all the way up."

"Good. Don't forget to leave your business card in the jar. If you win, you get free coffee for a week."

Dennis nodded and dropped it in the jar. An awkward silence followed before he extended his arm for a handshake.

"A handshake?" she laughed as she shook his hand, both of them holding onto the shake and looking into each other's eyes far longer than either expected to.

"She had to be flirting with me," Dennis said to himself as he climbed back into his SUV.

Or did she?

She couldn't possibly be interested in an older married man with three kids. She probably was that way with everyone to ensure bigger tips.

Or was she?

He had been there enough times over the years to know that wasn't the case. And yet, he remained unsure. It didn't matter much either way he decided, since he was unlikely to act on it even if she was interested.

That's when his phone buzzed with a text message from a number he didn't recognize. The text read, *"Do I make this bikini look cute?"* There was a picture attached of Erika in what looked like the stock room, wearing a string bikini with a white top and navy bottom. Truth be told, there wasn't much to it, but what there was looked spectacular. He was so caught off guard that he fumbled with his phone until he dropped it on the floor of his car. He felt around with his foot and then reached down with one hand while he drove, the car swerving with every effort. Finally, he grasped the phone just as the sound of a car horn blared. He looked up in a panic and found himself driving head on towards a car on the other side of the road. He yanked the wheel back to his side towards an elderly man who stared directly into his eyes in horror. Dennis locked up the brakes on his Range Rover and everything suddenly went dark.

Chapter 3
The Second Chance Station

Al came to in a suffocating, cold and wet mist that had surrounded him on all sides, before he realized all he needed to do was stand up to escape it. He bounced up, light as a feather and felt the best he had felt physically in decades. Scanning the area for miles in every direction, he saw nothing but clouds and bright blue skies. No buildings. No people. Nothing. And then, finally, a car. Al heard it before he saw it, a red Ferrari 308 GTB, just like in the old television series Magnum P.I. But Magnum wasn't behind the wheel.

"Al. Welcome!" the man said.

Al studied him intensely, wondering exactly where he was and who this man was. He was African American. Late 50's. Grey speckled in with his dark hair. His voice was deep, booming almost, and he was sporting a Hawaiian shirt, shorts with flip flops and a Detroit Tigers baseball cap. Al had entered into some surreal world he didn't understand.

"You look different on TV, Magnum."

"I get that a lot," the man smiled before

adding, "you've lived quite a life. I thought this would be more fun and fitting for a man of your stature."

"Do I know you?" Al asked.

"No. But I know you. We have been eagerly awaiting your arrival."

"And where exactly am I? And who are you?"

"My apologies. That was rude of me. I'm Gabriel. Archangel Gabriel to be precise."

"Does that mean I'm in heaven?"

"Sort of."

"Sort of? Do I need to pass a test first? I thought you said I'd lived quite a life?"

"You have. And yes, it's sort of a test. But don't worry. I'm certain you will pass with flying colors. I'll explain on the way. Hop in."

Not seeing much of an alternative and the fact that he was about to ride in a Ferrari for the first time convinced him to climb in.

"In answer to your first question, this is the Second Chance Station. Think of it as a town in the suburbs of heaven. I run it."

"Is this the place where people who screwed their lives up are sent?" Al asked.

"The opposite actually. It's where people that have lived a good life, are sent to collect their reward."

"Reward? Don't most people live a good life? I mean, no one's perfect including me, but aren't most people inherently good?"

"The majority are good, yes, but this place is for those that lived a special life."

"What exactly made mine special?"

"Too many different things to recount right now. But how bout I show you instead?" Gabriel said as they sped off through the clouds.

***

They came around a bend and burst through a cloud, revealing what looked like a stadium in the far off distance. It's brick facade, plentiful advertising signs and lights were unmistakable to a lifelong fan. They were pulling into Citi Field, the home of the New York Mets. Gabriel waved to the man at the guard shack and whizzed into a spot by the VIP entrance.

"This is some dream," Al remarked. "We're at Citi Field!"

"Everyone sees what they want to see," Gabriel answered.

"What if I wanted to see a strip club and some hot totties?"

"If you wanted to see that, you would."

"A fair point," Al nodded.

They walked down the tunnel straight inside of the main entrance and Gabriel pulled open the door to the First Data Club, the swanky club for elite ticket holders located behind home plate. Bright lights, chrome patterns on the ceiling. Food stations that ranged from shaved steak to cups of soup and vinegar cucumber salads. There was also a fully stocked, private bar. It was crowded.

"Who are all these people?" Al asked.

"People like you."

"Mets fans?"

"Some of them."

"And the others?"

"See something different."

"Any Yankees fans in here that I can go choke out?"

"Yankees fans go to a different place."

"In the basement I hope."

"A different place," Gabriel smiled.

"Is that Keanu Reeves?" Al asked, pointing to a man by the bar.

"Yes."

"But he's not dead."

"Well, he won't be in five days."

"What do you mean by that?"

"He's lived a good life like you. He will have the same opportunity."

"You're pretty cryptic with your answers, Gabriel."

Al was growing frustrated. He had never had any patience for bullshit.

"I don't mean to be."

"Then give me some straight answers."

"What do you want to know?"

"Where am I? What am I doing here? Where am I going? And what is this reward you talked about? Those are for starters."

They continued walking down the corridor, through the Mets locker room, and into a film room. There were two rows of cushioned, theatre-style chairs with the Mets logo emblazoned on the headrest and speakers on the sides.

"Have a seat," Gabriel offered.

"I'd prefer to stand."

"You'll want to be sitting once I answer your questions."

Chapter 4
The Rules & the Reward

"Water?" Gabriel asked as he opened the floor fridge.

"Got any whiskey?" Al responded.

"We've got everything. But I think you'll want to have a clear head for what you're about to do," Gabriel answered as he seated himself next to him.

"And what am I about to do?"

"Well, I already told you where you are," Gabriel stated, rising again and standing in front of Al, who had somehow managed to look uncomfortable in a very comfortable chair.

"The Second Chance Station?" Al asked.

"Correct."

"Is this place like the lobby of heaven?"

"Not exactly. Think of it as Grand Central Station, with trains coming in and going out in every direction."

"I'm in New York City?"

"Not exactly," Gabriel answered. "Maybe Penn Station is a better comparison. With trains coming in and going out, some to areas outside of New York. And sometimes...people are put back on the same train they came in on."

"I'm not following you."

"In my effort to be subtle, I'm afraid I'm not doing a very good job explaining. Let me ask you this. Have you ever wished you could go back and re-experience some of the best days of your life? Your first kiss. Being the hero in the homecoming game. Meeting your wife for the first time. Returning to American soil after a tour in Vietnam..."

"Sure," Al admitted.

"How about days you had regrets? Ever wish you could go back and fix them?"

"I guess."

"What about if you could go back and change events from history for the greater good?"

"Can't say that I've ever given much thought to that, since it isn't likely to happen."

"But what if it could?" Gabriel asked, his eyes widening with a knowing smile.

Al rubbed his thumb and forefinger over his chin in thought. "And you're such a person that could make that happen?"

"I am," Gabriel answered before adding, "You've been given a great gift, Al. Because of the way you lived your life, you're being given the opportunity to go back and re-live any five days from it."

"Any five days," Al repeated.

"Correct. They could be days from when you were a little kid. Could be yesterday. Or somewhere in between."

"But what do you mean by go back? As in watch myself like a movie of my life?"

"Definitely not a movie. You will be an active participant," Gabriel assured him. "You go back as yourself in whatever age the days you choose occur. The only difference is, you go back then armed with what you know now."

"And I can do things differently if I want?"

"That's the idea. Although I imagine on some of the days you won't want to change a thing."

Al stood up and paced back and forth across the room in deep thought. "How do I even choose? I'm 77 years old. There's a lot of days to choose from."

"Understood. We have something for you in your room that should help you with that."

"My room? Am I sleeping on 1st base or in the dugout?"

"Why don't you follow me?" Gabriel said with a smile.

The room opened into a long tunnel that in the old days, would have been dark, dusty and cold, but with today's modern stadiums, was bright and airy, almost nostalgic, with pictures of former Mets greats lining the walls. Tom "Terrific" Seaver. Dwight "Doc" Gooden.

Keith "Mex" Hernandez. Gary "Kid" Carter. And the iconic picture of Mookie Wilson sprinting up the first base line as a bouncing ball was about to find its way underneath the glove of Red Sox first baseman, Bill Buckner. At the end of the hallway were the steps up to the Mets dugout, followed by a few more steps to the field itself. Al motioned with his head and pointed to the infield.

"Go ahead," Gabriel said.

Al stepped into the batter's box with his imaginary bat held high, his bent trail arm shoulder high. He swung and watched the imaginary ball sail toward the left field corner before taking off down the first base line. He was moving pretty good for his age, whistling around first, and then second, pushing off the inside of the base as he headed for third. Al showed no signs of slowing up as he turned for home. When he was a few feet away he *slid*, a hook slide, touching the base with his hand.

He laughed as he sat in a cloud of dust and dirt, 77 years young, feeling as though he was 10 again. "Do you have laundry up here?"

"Of course," Gabriel responded, amused. "C'mon."

Al jumped to his feet and followed Gabriel through the outfield, pausing to take in his surroundings for a little while longer. This had to be the coolest thing he had ever experienced he determined. Gabriel held open the door to the bullpen and although he couldn't explain why, he suddenly felt a little like he was about to step into a cornfield in Iowa.

He walked through the door and was met with a kaleidoscope of colors that quickly dissolved and left him speechless. When his eyes refocused, he found they were standing outside the white picket fence in front of his house. The fence was a little worn and the gate needed to be adjusted. The house itself was also in need of a good power washing and the garden need to be weeded and cut back. He definitely didn't have the green thumb that his wife had. He just hadn't realized it until that very moment. But make no mistake about it, the house was still a beautiful southern colonial with a front porch that ran the full length of it.

"You coming?" Gabriel asked as he held open the gate.

"When you said my room, I thought you meant like a hotel or something," Al answered awkwardly.

"We wanted you to be comfortable."

They entered the foyer and Gabriel continued into the kitchen. "The fridge is fully stocked if you're hungry or thirsty."

"Thanks," he responded before adding, "So how does this work?"

"How does what work?"

"The days. How do I choose them and how do I let you know?"

"As I mentioned, I left you a little gift in your living room that will help you choose. As for how you let me know, write them on a piece of paper, stick it into an envelope and put it in your mailbox. You don't need to have exact dates. Just descriptions will be enough."

"One more question. If I change something, does it change things just for that day, or every day that follows?"

"Depends what it is. If it's something insignificant, it probably won't have any impact at all, but other things...could affect the rest of your life, not to mention other people's lives. So be careful. Each major decision you make could have a ripple of effects."

"Got it."

"Piece of advice. As I've said, you've truly been given a great gift. One that not many people get, but nearly everyone would want. Don't stress over it. Enjoy it."

Al nodded with a bit of uncertainty. "And what happens at the end of the five days? Do I get sent back here? Or somewhere else?"

"That really depends on you," Gabriel answered. "I'll see you eventually."

"What's that supposed to mean?"

"Don't read too much into it. I simply mean I'll see you eventually, whether it be days or years is kind of up to you."

Al walked to the living room and saw a DVD sitting on the coffee table. The label read, "Al Sokratis 1942 - 2019". He shook his head with the realization that he didn't own a DVD player, until he noticed they had provided him with one. He turned on the TV, and fumbled with the disc, inserting it upside down and having it spit back out, before he finally got it to play. He dimmed the lights as if he was ready to watch a classic movie, which he kind of was, and sat down on his couch.

"Care to join me?" he asked Gabriel.

Gabriel thought it over for a moment. It would be a bit unusual, but why not?

"I've always got time to watch a good movie," he answered.

Chapter 5
Max Carter

Others might have disagreed, but "amazing" was the only word that came to mind whenever Al found himself staring at a late autumn afternoon where the skies were grey, the air crisp, and the temperature required a sweatshirt but nothing beyond that. He pulled into the driveway at his high school and drove around to the back where the football field proudly stood. It was early and there was still the morning dew on the lines that had been freshly painted on, although the surprisingly warm November sun was doing its best to dry everything out.

Although neither program was particularly strong, the Stonington, Connecticut-Westerly, Rhode Island Thanksgiving Day football game was one of the longest standing in the nation. The rivalry between two schools in neighboring states separated by three miles and a river began in 1911 but moved to Thanksgiving in 1913. With the exception of a gap left during World War I, they had played every year since with Stonington holding a slight edge in the series going into the 1961 game. With the 1960 game ending in a 6-6 tie, the 1961 game had added importance in the yearly bragging rights after a year of "kissing their sisters".

Al entered the locker room through the back of the school expecting it to be empty and quiet seeing as it was still three hours before the game, but he heard voices echoing off the concrete walls and floor. He turned the corner and saw three of his teammates stuffing another student into a locker. The two offensive linemen and the middle linebacker weren't big by modern standards, but were sizable for 1961. The poor kid in question was literally about half their size. Al recognized him from English class. Max Carter was a bit quiet and introverted, and although he couldn't put his finger on exactly why, there was something about his mannerisms and pattern of speech that made Al feel as though Max was always one step ahead of everyone else.

"What's going on, fellas?" Al asked.

If literally anyone else had asked, the three football players would have ignored him and simply carried on with their business, but Al commanded respect. He wasn't the biggest guy on the team, but he was tall, strong and had an air of quiet confidence about him that exuded toughness. And no one was daring enough find out just how tough.

"Hey, Al. We caught this guy sniffing about the locker room," the biggest of them answered. He was broad shouldered, not fat, not exactly chiseled either, but his flat top haircut made him look menacing.

"I wasn't sniffing..." Max began to protest before realizing it was a futile argument to have.

"He wasn't sniffing," Al agreed. "He was here to meet me. The guy is an offensive football tactical genius. You should see some of the plays and formations he has in that notebook of his."

One of the other players ripped the notebook out of Max's unwilling hands and began flipping through it. He gave a shrug of approval as he showed it to his teammate, who nodded as well.

"Sorry," Flat Top said without a great deal of sincerity as he slapped the notebook into Max's chest. Turning to the other guys he said, "C'mon, let's go see if any of the cheerleaders have shown up yet."

Once they had left, Al motioned for Max to grab a seat on the bench. "Let's have a look at these things."

"How did you know I was diagramming plays and formations?" Max asked.

"You're at every practice sitting in the stands with your notebook. It was either that or you're studying to become a sketch artist."

Max flipped the pad open and the drawings looked like something out of *A Beautiful Mind*. X's, O's, arrows and dashes drowned pages upon pages of paper.

"4 wide receiver sets? I'll be running for my life," Al laughed.

"You'll be running for touchdowns. The other team would have no choice but to stretch and cover which will open up tons of gaps."

"And what if they blitz instead?"

"Then pull the tight end and leave a back in the backfield to pick it up. Beat them with a quick slant and they won't blitz again."

"It is interesting. Most teams aren't designed to stop this. They pack the box to stop the run because most teams don't pass much."

"The difference is that you can throw a ball. I've seen you chuck it 70 yards in practice."

"72," Al winked.

One of the three players from before charged back into the room at that moment. "Charlie thinks he can pick the lock to the girls locker room and a few of the cheerleaders are changing in there!"

Al jumped up. It was a bit out of character for him, but he was after all, a high school boy. "You coming?" he asked Max.

Max hesitated for only the briefest of moments before he determined that he might never get another chance to see a naked woman. Lord knows he hadn't seen one to that point.

They arrived outside the double doors that led to the promised land just as Charlie slipped his father's new VISA credit card into the gap and pulled it towards him until the bolt released. The boys quietly, or what they thought was quietly, snuck into the shower area and found girls in varying arrays of undress. A couple were in towels. A couple in their under garments. One wore no clothes at all as she changed into her uniform.

Max's eyes grew wide as saucers as the girl screamed and the other boys scattered. He was frozen, staring at her, until Al realized he was still back there and spun him around by the shoulder. None of them stopped running until they reached the boys locker room, laughing hysterically to the point of tears coming down their cheeks.

"What are you idiots doing?!" their coach bellowed. "Certainly not focusing on the game! And I better not find out you were sneaking into the girls locker room again!"

Stan Bocanegra was a local legend. Taught PE at the high school for 35 years, was an Assistant Coach for 10 and had been the head coach for 25. PE classes were extended versions of practice in which players could work on weaknesses against some unsuspecting female editor of the yearbook subbing in as a defensive lineman. The 1961 Thanksgiving Day game would also be Stan's last, having announced his retirement at the beginning of the season. As gruff as he could be at times, his players loved him and wanted to win it for him.

Down 6-0 at halftime, Al approached his coach with an innovative and slightly irregular idea.

"A four wide receiver set??" the old coach bellowed. "We don't have *one* receiver who can catch a ball. What's adding three more going to do?"

"It's going to stretch the defense," Al reasoned. "We've got plenty of time. If they drop off, I'll run it. If they blitz, we'll catch them with quick hitters. If they play it straight, I'll throw over the top."

"It isn't the worst idea I've ever heard," Stan admitted reluctantly. He respected Al's football acumen enough to let him have such input. Al would need to save the conversation about who actually came up with the idea until after the game—if it worked.

They broke out the "spread" offense on their first series of the second half and the Westerly players scrambled to cover. Players were dropping, moving forward and moving wide all at the same time. Al snapped the ball and saw one of his wide receivers all alone near midfield. He hit him in stride and he went untouched into the end zone. On the next series, he took a two-step drop before he saw nothing but green grass in front of him as he darted up the middle of the field, the Westerly defense parting like the Red Sea before him. Forty-five yards later, he was deep in Westerly territory before being pushed out of bounds. When they blitzed on the next play, he hit one of his receivers streaking across the middle of the field for another seventeen yards. He followed it with a post route and a touchdown as the Westerly team and coaching staff began to argue and scream at each other. They were in complete chaos.

When the whistle blew signaling the end of the game, Stonington had a 16-6 victory and their fans, lined four deep by the fence and overflowing from the bleachers, poured onto the field. Al soon found himself surrounded by people, but was seeking out one in particular.

"You were right, you sonuvagun!" he told Max as he gave him a bear hug. "C'mon back to the locker room with us."

"What?"

"You've earned it. C'mon."

Stan had tears in his eyes when he addressed the team for the last time post game. "I can't tell you what an honor it's been to coach you young men for the last four years, and work at this school for the last 35. I've spent more than half my life in these halls, and I thank you from the bottom of my heart for your effort today and for sending me out in my last game with a win. Now, I wish I could take the credit for this win, but that second half strategy came curtesy of your captain. Game ball—Al Sokratis!"

"Coach. I know I speak for all of us when I say the privilege has been ours. You've taught us not just how to play football, but how to be better men. And even when we have failed at one or the other of those things, you stood by us and supported us. Couldn't be happier to send you out with a win. You deserve it. But I can't take the credit for today. The innovative offense comes from this guy right here," Al said as he grabbed Max and yanked him into the circle. "Game ball—Max Carter!"

The team roared as they lifted Max high into the air and tossed him up and down. The smile on his face lasted long after his feet were firmly back on the ground.

"What are you up to tonight?" Al asked.

"Just Thanksgiving dinner with the family," Max answered with a shrug.

"I mean after that. Jenny Slater is having a party."

"I wasn't invited."

"Consider yourself invited. I'll pick you up around 8:00."

"I mean Jenny is choice, but I don't know."

"What don't you know?"

"Today has been arguably the best day of my life."

"C'mon really?"

"Yeah. You may find this hard to believe, but my life isn't very exciting. And what is it they say about gamblers? Get out while the gettin is good?"

"They also say when you're on a hot streak, ride it as long as you can, because they don't happen very often," Al responded with a smile.

* * *

"Whatever happened to Max?" Gabriel asked from Al's living room couch in the sky.

"Became a student coach at Notre Dame, then stayed on as a GA. Eventually won three Super Bowls as the Offensive Coordinator for the Dallas Cowboys."

"You ever hear from him after high school?"

"My wife and I were guests of his in the owner's suite for all three of the Super Bowls," Al smiled as he pointed to the framed tickets on the wall.

"You changed his life that day."

"The cream eventually rises to the top. He

would have made his own way."

"You don't know that."

Al shrugged. "I was just trying to be a good person."

"That's more than most people do," Gabriel assured him. "Trust me as someone who has seen it all."

"Worked out ok for me too. I ended up marrying his cousin."

Chapter 6
The Battle of Minh Thanh

Rich Cosgrove was Al's best friend in high school and theirs was an interesting friendship. While Al was athletic, measured in his responses and quiet unless he needed to be otherwise, Rich was as smart and funny as he was unathletic and unmotivated. Al commanded respect. Rich neither required it nor gave it to anyone. He was the person with razor sharp wit that always said the exact thing you wanted to say or the thing you wished you had thought of at the time, instead of two hours later.

When Al and Rich were at a party attempting to drown Al's sorrows over his girlfriend breaking up with him since he was going away to college, and they happened to run into her, she commented how drunk they were.

"Yes, we are. And you're ugly. But tomorrow we'll be sober," Rich stated, borrowing from Winston Churchill.

There was also the time when a boy made fun of a girl who was a bit "eccentric" in her clothing choices and Rich defended her, "This coming from a guy wearing spit shined penny loafers with the pennies in them and a jacket that looks like the liner to a much nicer jacket. Could you be less creative and unique?"

And when someone laughed at a friend of his for scoring a 68 on a Math test. "He's in Calculus. You're taking Senior Math. I've got a 95 in Senior Math and I haven't done a thing all year. Patting yourself on the back for having an 80 in that class is like giving yourself a compliment for not driving over your own foot in your driveway."

But Rich didn't insult people just to insult them. He insulted those that deserved it, in an effort to defend those that either couldn't or wouldn't defend themselves. Usually it had a disarming effect, and most people laughed, but his mouth occasionally got him into trouble when someone took it the wrong way. Al didn't mind having to bail him out of a few sticky wickets though because Rich's loyalty and friendship was second to none.

He was always the first person to jump into a scrap for a friend. The person you could call to pick you up when your car broke down without a word of complaint or any expectation of gas money or you repaying the favor. And because of all that and more, when Rich found himself drafted for Conscription in the spring of

1966, Al knew there was only one thing for him to do — he enlisted.

While Rich was finishing basic training before heading to Vietnam, Al was graduating from college. His degree made him more likely to receive a more out of the way job like going to Officer's Training School or becoming a clerk in charge of sending soldiers home, but he requested to be sent to join his friend in the 1st Infantry Division. Following training at Fort Riley, Kansas, he was then sent to Vietnam as well, but he never told Rich he was coming. Not that he could have reached him if he had wanted to.

Being a member of the 1st Infantry was like having courtside seats to war. Their motto was *No Mission too difficult. No sacrifice too great.*

Al joined the 1st in An Loc, South Vietnam in late June of that year. When he tracked Rich down, he walked up behind him and gave him a shove in the back. Rich wheeled around, ready to fight, when he realized his old friend was standing before him.

"What the hell are you doing here?!! Did you get drafted?" Rich exclaimed.

"Nope," Al shook his head.

"You enlisted?"

"That is generally the other way one ends up here."

"You dumb bastard," Rich laughed. "You do realize as a college grad you could pretty much have your pick of jobs and platoons?"

"Someone had to come save your ass," Al smiled.

"Boys," Rich proclaimed in a grand effort to garner everyone's attention, "this here guy is the dumbest man to ever graduate from Notre Dame. Instead of getting drafted, he enlisted. And instead of taking a cush clerk position, he elected to join the 1st!"

They roared, drumming on the tops of their helmets as Rich pulled him in for a manly hug. "I can't believe you're here."

Two weeks later, on July 9, 1966, members of the 1st Infantry Division were sent as "bait" from An Loc toward Minh Thanh on a mostly deserted road. The idea was to send some supply trucks in a caravan with only light armored protection onto Minh Thanh Road headed towards the airfield for the purpose of drawing out the heavy Viet Cong presence that was in the area. When the Viet Cong attempted to ambush the caravan, they would be ambushed by a much larger onslaught of firepower from both the ground and air.

Even with the support, waiting to be ambushed in the middle of nowhere was an uneasy feeling. It seemed as though some of them would be unnecessary casualties in order to win the battle. Al just hoped he wouldn't be one of them.

* * *

The first shot ripped through the windshield on their Jeep and exploded into the driver's chest. He was likely dead on contact, but Al couldn't afford to find out for certain. He was in the passenger seat and had to grab the wheel, pull his fallen squad member to the side, and climb over him into the driver's seat. If they stopped, they would all be dead.

He punched the gas and the Jeep rumbled on dodging mortar and rifle fire until one of the Viet Cong took out one of the rear tires, sending the truck into a tailspin. It flipped onto its side, dumping equipment, supplies and the men in the back onto the dusty road.

As they scrambled for cover behind the truck, a couple more were taken out by rifle shots.

"Where was the support?" Al wondered. But what had seemed like ten minutes was in reality about 35 seconds. War had a way of doing something no doctor or scientist had yet found a way to do—stop time.

The road was littered with slain soldiers and as the dust began to dissipate, Al saw one of them in the road next to the vehicle in front of them. As his eyes began to clear he saw it was

Rich, his leg shattered, crawling towards the vehicle, shooting his gun aimlessly into the air.

With no time to waste, Al raced toward him, hunched down low, bullets whistling by his head. Making it back behind his overturned truck would be nearly impossible, so he grabbed Rich, threw him over his shoulder and dove into the tall grass on the side of the road.

"Fuck, it hurts!" Rich screamed, grabbing his leg.

"I'll be back," Al said as he went off to check on the others.

By that time, Al had figured where the attack was emanating about seventy-five yards northeast of where they were. To buy himself some time, he removed a grenade from his waistband, pulled the pin, and chucked it in that direction. It was a toss that would have made his old coach proud. The grenade exploded just as it hit and two bodies flew into the air at impact.

He reached the fallen soldiers in his platoon and began dragging them to safety. Four of them in total. But on the 4th one, he felt a sharp pain in his lower back, as if someone had smashed him directly with a baseball bat. He stumbled to the grass where Rich was as planes stormed in overhead and troops surrounded the Viet Cong on all sides. Help had arrived.

"You ok, buddy?" he asked, grimacing in

pain himself.

"Look at my leg! There's nothing left of it! I'll never be able to run again!"

"I wouldn't worry too much about it," Al responded, using his shirt as a tourniquet to stop the bleeding. "You were never very fast to begin with."

"Fuck you," Rich laughed through the pain.

"Other than that, are you ok?"

"So Mrs. Lincoln, other than that, how did you enjoy the play? Do I look ok??" Rich asked.

"To be honest, you look at little shorter."

"You have the worst bedside manner of all time," Rich grimaced.

* * *

"And you were sent home with a Purple Heart after that day," Gabriel said.

"Which I didn't deserve. I was only there for two weeks."

"You didn't even have to be there at all. You weren't drafted. You certainly didn't need to be on the front lines."

"I would have been drafted sooner or later."

"You were a hero. You saved 5 lives that day and got shot in the process. An inch to the right and you'd have been paralyzed."

Al shrugged. "But I wasn't."

"What happened to Rich?" Gabriel asked.

"He made it home, but was never the same mentally. He lost his leg below the knee and withdrew further and further. One day, nearly twenty years after Vietnam, he put a pistol in his mouth and killed himself."

"And you blamed yourself."

"I should have been there for him."

"How could you have known?" Gabriel asked.

"He once told me he wished I had let him die out there on that road," Al answered, fidgeting with a coaster on the coffee table.

"That was his problem, not yours. You gave him a second chance at life. It was his choice to give it away."

Chapter 7
And the Runner Up is...

There were three kinds of high school teachers. Those that were brilliant, but unable to teach or relate to the students, and as a result, generally not well liked. Those that were popular, but not well respected because they were too concerned with being well liked to actually teach anything. And then the smattering few that managed to be both popular and well respected because they could teach *and* were able to relate to the students. Al was one of the smattering few.

"How many solutions are there in a quadratic equation?" he asked a room full of half-asleep students.

It was a full thirty seconds before someone finally responded. "Two?" a girl in the front of the room answered quietly. She was plain looking, shy, with glasses, an argyle sweater with khaki pants and her hair pulled up in a bun.

"Are you asking me or telling me?" Al asked.

"Telling?"

"Sounds like you're asking. Have confidence in yourself."

"Two!" she said forcefully this time.

"Not necessarily," he answered, quickly deflating her new found confidence. "It could have one, two or no real number solutions. Now what's the easiest way to solve a quadratic equation?"

"By factoring it," a boy answered. He was wearing Sambas with jeans; a terrible look in any era, but more readily accepted in the 80's.

"What if you can't factor it?"

"You use the quadratic formula," the boy answered proudly.

"And what is that?"

"Negative b, plus or minus the square root of b squared minus $4ac$ over $2a$."

"Excellent, Mr. Evans."

"Mr. S, no offense, but when are we ever going to need this stuff?" another boy asked. He was tall and clean shaven, but sloppily neat with an untucked button down and shaggy hair. "It's not like someone's going to ask us to solve a quadratic equation on a job interview."

"Probably not," Al acknowledged, "but someday you might want to re-do your patio and you'll need to know how many square feet it is or what angles to cut the stone at."

"I'll hire someone."

"Here's the thing that no one will tell you,

Mr. Jones. Math teaches you to be organized. To work systematically to solve problems. And everyone needs to know how to do that."

"I'm going to invent a calculator that will solve quadratic equations for me," Mr. Jones countered.

"You going to carry this calculator around with you?" Al asked, curiously.

"I'm going to invent a mobile phone that has a calculator built into it that solves quadratic equations," Mr. Evans offered.

"Mobile phones only work if they're plugged into a cigarette lighter in your car. And they cost about $2,000 a minute to use, stupido," Mr. Jones shot back.

"Let me ask you something, Mr. Jones," Al started, "How are you going to invent a calculator that solves quadratic equations when you don't even know how to solve them?"

Both boys went silent for a moment as the class laughed.

"Why you gotta crap in my cornflakes, Mr. S?" Mr. Jones responded at last.

"It's better than peeing in your porridge," Al answered.

"That's nasty."

"So Mr. S, you going to watch the space shuttle launch this morning?" Mr. Evans asked.

"You really are a stupido," Mr. Jones said.

"What?"

"Why are you reminding him of something he didn't get to do?"

Al chuckled. "It's fine. Really. And yes, I plan to watch it."

"Are you jealous?" Mr. Evans asked.

"Maybe a little," Al admitted. "But I'm happy for her at the same time."

The bell rang and the students sprung from their seats quicker than usual. A man suddenly appeared in the doorway. Sturdy build. Muscular. Athletic. Wearing a polo shirt that had "Stonington Football" embroidered on the chest.

"Welcome back, buddy," the man said. Joe Benedetto had been Al's lifelong friend and played on the state championship team with him back in 1960.

"Thanks, big man. Good to be back."

"You didn't miss much while you were off pretending to be an astronaut. Just a crappy football season. And we lost to Westerly to put a nice exclamation point on it."

"The team was young. Next year will be our year," Al reassured him.

"I sure hope so. Say, you got a minute? Beth is setting up for the play tomorrow night and needs some help moving the scaffolding."

"Sure. No problem. I'm off this period anyway. As long as I get to watch the shuttle launch."

"She's got a TV in the auditorium hooked up to the satellite feed. Tough morning for you, huh?" Joe said as they walked down the corridor.

"Why do you say that?"

"Well, I mean, to be so close to something incredible like that and to not get to do it. It's got to be soul crushing."

"Are you trying to cheer me up?"

"I'm just saying...if it was me, I don't know if I'd even be able to get out of bed in the morning."

"Thanks for the pick me up, buddy."

Joe smiled as he pulled open one of the double doors to the auditorium and held it open for Al, who didn't even notice that the entire room was packed. As soon as he stepped inside, the auditorium exploded in cheers. Current students. Former students. Teachers. Friends. Al's parents. His wife and son. It took him a minute to realize what was happening, as he walked towards his wife. A sign above the stage read "WELCOME HOME TO STONINGTON'S FAVORITE SON AND ASTRONAUT".

The man on the stage was the school's Principal. He was tall and thin, with salt and pepper hair, sporting a light grey suit with a white shirt and royal blue tie. "Ladies and gentlemen. Longtime teacher, coach, and Hall of Fame athlete, Stonington's own, Al Sokratis!"

The crowd erupted once more.

"Being friends with you in this town is like being the red headed step child of the family," Joe shook his head.

A projector screen on the stage showed the shuttle preparing for takeoff. Al kissed his wife and gave her a hug.

"It's good to have you home," she said.

"It's good to be home."

"Sad?"

"Nah. I'm good. Maybe a little," he relented with a smile as he high-fived his son.

The Teacher in Space Program had been instituted by Ronald Reagan in 1984, with the idea of sending a teacher into space to teach lessons to America's students. The goal of the program was to honor teachers and inspire students to learn more about math, science and space exploration. In all, more than 11,000 people applied to be the first non-astronaut in space. From that pool, 114 semifinalists were selected, representing all 50 states, before a panel chose the 10 finalists that headed to the Johnson Space Center in Houston for additional interviews and testing.

Al emerged as one of the two finalists, a great story as a Vietnam war hero, turned high school teacher in the small Connecticut coastal town he grew up in, but he lost out to another high school teacher from New England, an ordinary person with an infectious personality that the program thought would play well with kids while teaching lessons from Space. If Al was disappointed, he never let on to that fact, saying it was an "honor" to have made it as far as he did. He even became close friends with the teacher selected along with the crew of the Challenger while training as the backup teacher for four months. Watching them ascend into the sky that morning was sure to be a conflicting moment for him. Excited and proud for his friends, but sad that he wasn't with them. It was a little like being the last person cut from the USA's Olympic hockey team's Miracle on Ice.

"Four...three...two...one...and lift off. Lift off of the 25th Space Shuttle mission and it has cleared the tower..." the announcer said as millions cheered from schools and homes throughout the country.

But when an explosion occurred 73 seconds into the flight, the auditorium went eerily silent. Everyone knew something was wrong, but it wasn't until the announcer said, "Flight controllers here looking carefully at the situation. Obviously, a major malfunction," that their worst fears were confirmed.

Al stood in shock, staring at the screen before him, unable to utter a single word, even after his wife burst into tears and ran from the room.

"I'm guessing he's not jealous now," Mr. Evans whispered to Mr. Jones in the audience. "What? Too soon?" he asked as Mr. Jones shook his head.

Al eventually snapped out his shock enough to find his wife sobbing uncontrollably in the corridor.

"Are you ok?" he asked. He was confused. She had only met the seven members of the crew one time. "I can't believe that happened."

"Yes, it's awful, but that's not why I'm crying. I'm crying because it could have been you. It could have been you..." she kept repeating.

Chapter 8
In a Mere Instant

More often than not people fell in love before eventually falling out of it. Once in a while, people fell in lust before learning to love each other. This was such a story.

Lisa Waters first met Jimmy Sokratis while she was waiting tables at a dive sports bar in town. Jimmy was visiting his parents in the off season of his attempt to play professional hockey. Following a promising high school and youth hockey career, he had several offers to play in college, but bypassed them and headed straight to the pros. After dreaming of skating onto the ice in front of 19,000 people at Madison Square Garden, he landed with a thud in the American Hockey League, playing for the New York Rangers affiliate, the New Haven Nighthawks, playing before 2,500 fans while traveling to exotic locations like Binghamton, Syracuse, Rochester, Utica and Portland, Maine. In his heart of hearts, he knew he wasn't good enough, but he hung onto the dream as long as he could, because it enabled him to avoid the real world for just a little while longer.

He was handsome, probably too much so for his own good, because it enabled him to slide by on his looks and charm his entire life, instead of actually working to get ahead. Eventually it caught up to him, as he found himself without a college degree, unqualified to do much of anything except manual labor, which he found beneath him after years of being idolized.

But for Lisa, Jimmy was a welcome respite from the gin-soaked, ass slapping gamblers that staggered in daily to watch the horse races at Belmont and Aqueduct. Even on his downward spiral, he was funny and charming. Most bars had policies against employees drinking with the patrons, but this bar encouraged it and when Jimmy asked her to join him for drinks at the end of her shift, she was only all too happy to do so.

Several shots and multiple drinks later, they ended up back at Lisa's apartment. Her roommate looked up from watching TV in the living room as they fell into the room, realizing it was her cue to head to bed. It wasn't the first time it had happened, but it was the last, as Sammy was conceived that very night.

Their marriage was one of decided inconvenience. Him a 22 year old minor league hockey player with unrealized dreams. Her a 19 year old waitress who was too young to take good care of herself, much less anyone else. And yet, they stayed together for more than ten years, growing in appreciation and love as time passed. If they fought, it was usually over money, or a lack of it, but as long as both of them were working, they managed to get by.

Al and his wife were always around to get Sammy off the bus and watch him until his parents came home which made life easier for all. His hockey playing days limited to over-30 men's leagues now, Jimmy finished his shift at the stone yard around 5:00 before heading to his parents for dinner and to bring Sammy home. Lisa finished her shift several hours later and would come home to find both of her "men" asleep on the couches.

She was an absentee mom more out of necessity than anything, but a lovely person when she was around. Lisa had an enormous heart, which was obvious the first time anyone met her, and kids were intuitive. Sammy loved her for that. He loved his dad as well, even though he had always sensed his father was angry at the world for how his life had turned out.

Overall, their family was not unlike millions of others. Stressful, hard-working, and held together by the pliable bonds of love, that were at times stretched to their limits. Occasionally, those bonds were broken by a cruel twist of fate.

One night, after working a double, Lisa was offered a ride home from a co-worker. She knew her friend had a few drinks at the end of her shift, but didn't realize how many until the woman started playing Pac-Man with the dotted line in the middle of the road. The last thing either of them saw, as Lisa frantically reached for the steering wheel, was the blinding light of the car approaching from the other side of the road.

***

A knock on the door after midnight was never a good thing. No one ever delivered the news of you winning the Publisher's Clearinghouse Sweepstakes at that time. No one offered you a new job then. No one stopped by to wish you a happy birthday. Or invited you to go on vacation with them. Those things could all wait until morning.

So when Jimmy saw the police officer on his front steps at that time of night, he knew exactly what it was about. His reaction came in two waves. The first was the devastation at losing his wife. He dropped to his knees, overcome with emotion, until he realized he needed to pull himself together for the sake of his ten year old son, who had just lost his mother. The second was a wave of reality at having to survive and provide for his son on one low paying income. They had barely scraped by on two incomes. Doing so on one would be nearly impossible.

So he learned to cook, and took on a few extra shifts in order to keep them above water. But a burst water pump on his 1991 Ford Explorer, and ACL surgery for the family dog had set him way back financially with the holidays and Sammy's birthday just around the corner.

The one thing they had prided themselves in as a family was no matter how bleak things were financially, they would always find a way to make Sammy's birthday special. But his credit cards were already maxed out, and rent and bills were due within a week's time. He could have gone to his father for help, but he was already asking him to help pay his rent, which was an ego bursting moment for a 32 year old. Not to mention the fact that his parents already watched Sammy every single day while he worked.

With Sam at his parents, Jimmy grabbed a cheap bottle of whiskey from the cabinet and poured about four fingers worth into a plastic cup along with a few cubes of ice. When he finished that, he poured another. And then another. Until the 1/2 full bottle was empty. He followed that with the exceedingly poor decision of driving across town with the intent of robbing a store for cash. He went across town to minimize the chances of seeing anyone he knew, but things didn't work out exactly the way he planned.

He walked into the Mini-mart with his hand tucked inside his tattered rain jacket. He didn't own a gun, in fact, had never even shot one before, but he planned to pretend he had one now. The place was empty except for the mid-40's man behind the register whose eyes grew wide at the sight of a man in a ski mask with an alleged gun in his pocket approaching the register at two in the morning.

The man didn't hesitate. He reached under the counter and pulled out a shotgun as his dissuader. One didn't need to be as accurate with a shotgun, but they were harder to handle and slower to load. The slowness probably saved Jimmy's life and ended it at the same time.

As the man cocked it, Jimmy reached for the barrel and tried to wrestle it from him, but the man lunged over the counter and they tumbled to the floor. As they rolled around on the ground, the gun discharged and the struggle ended abruptly. Jimmy pushed the man off of him and could tell immediately that he was gone. He tried to revive him the best he could with CPR, calling 9-1-1 in between sets.

When the police arrived, Jimmy explained what happened. The man must have thought he was going to rob the place, when he was really only there to buy a few Slim Jim's and a soda. But when the cops found that he didn't have a penny in his pockets and the store cameras showed he had entered wearing a ski mask, they arrested him and charged him with murder.

Al was heartbroken, for his wife, for his grandson, and for himself. He felt like a failure for not having been able to help his son more than he had, but his focus needed to quickly turn to his grandson who he had to take in and raise on his own.

***

"So your son went to jail," Gabriel stated.

"When the cops looked at the tapes," Al nodded, "They saw intent for robbery. But he wasn't armed and they saw that the man pulled the gun on Jimmy before he had done anything, so they reduced the charge to manslaughter. He received eight years, but by the time he got out, his son, my grandson, was off at college. My one great regret in life, was that I was never able to reconnect them again, although lord knows I tried. And now it's too late."

"Is it?" Gabriel asked.

Chapter 9
The Mayor

After 38 years of teaching and coaching in the town he grew up in, Al Sokratis retired. A stint in Vietnam and more than three decades of public service had earned him a break. He planned to spend more time with his wife and grandson, in addition to taking up golf and following the Mets around Florida during spring training.

But just when he thought he was *out*, they pulled him back *in*. The town was in turmoil. The stock market had just crashed. The housing bubble was about to burst. Business and tourism had slowed to a crawl which drastically affected the tax base, putting the burden on each individual family. And yet, expenses remained. Schools needed repair and more modernized equipment to keep up with the other districts in the state. Teachers were due a salary bump. And the town was aging out. There were fewer students coming into the schools than were going out, and those that no longer had kids in the system didn't want to pay for those that did.

The two major party candidates for Mayor were more concerned with payoffs and supporting polar opposite platforms. One wanted to tax and spend. The other wanted to cut taxes and expenses. Neither would help balance the budget or solve the very real problems they faced.

Every inch of the Town Hall was jammed with people like wall-to-wall carpeting. It was standing room only as the two main party candidates squared off in a debate. Neither was impressive.

"In order to pay for the education budget, we need to implement a town tax to cover it," the first candidate said.

"We don't need another tax," the second one interjected. "What we need is to cut expenses. Education is important, but so is putting food on the table. Those are the difficult conversations we need to have."

Al raised his hand in the middle of the room. The moderator called on him. "Al?"

"Education is important. And I get that many of you no longer have kids in the system and don't want to pay into it any longer, but don't forget, that other people helped pay for your kids," Al stated. "From a practical standpoint, some of you may be looking to retire in a few years, and when that time comes, you'll want a robust housing market, and the only way you'll have that is by having a strong school system and low property taxes. So we need to invest in the school system, but raising taxes to pay for it isn't the answer. Connecticut is already one of the highest taxed states in the country. What we need to do is encourage small businesses to come here to help with our tax base. We should be more business friendly. Give tax breaks to restaurants, hotels and stores. Turn Stonington into a summer vacation destination. One of the dumbest things I've ever seen at the state level was putting in a long-term occupancy rental tax for people that rent a house or condo for less than 31 consecutive days. And now you guys are talking about an additional tax at the town level. Think about it. There is only so much people are willing to pay for a weekly rental. You throw an additional $500-$1000 on top of what they are already paying and one of two things will happen. Either people won't rent, or the owners will need to drop their prices, which means they'll make less money and in turn pay less in taxes. Not only should we not do it, but whoever gets elected should kick down the door at the Capitol Building in Hartford to talk them into removing the tax. Massachusetts has the same tax. So does Rhode Island. So undercut them and get people to come to Stonington and Mystic instead of Nantucket, the Vineyard and Block Island."

"Why aren't you up there, Al??" a man shouted.

"Get up there, Al!" another one chimed in.

"Al for Mayor!" a third said.

"Al! Al! Al!...." the crowd began chanting.

"Noooo. Noooo. Noooo. Noooo. No way, no how," Al countered. "I've done my time."

He was sworn in six months later.

Once in office, Al managed to keep all of his promises and then some. He pushed through the education budget without raising taxes in town. He encouraged businesses to move into the area by offering tax breaks. And he not only tossed out the occupancy tax in town, but managed to get the Governor to throw it out for the state as well.

He was best known, however, for creating the Big Family Program. It started small, where families could "adopt" another family by purchasing gift certificates for them that could be used at grocery stores, restaurants and hotels or housing rentals. The people that donated them could then deduct up to four times the amount from their taxable income. So at very little cost, they could help provide food or housing for another family for an entire year. It wasn't long before it spread to the state level. In the most basic sense, it shrank the state government by putting people in charge of helping people, instead of being told they had to do it. It was also "directed" help, meaning the gifts could only be used for certain necessities, which helped ensure the money was well spent.

"No one should go without basic necessities like housing and food," Al announced at his swearing in. "The key is encouraging people to help without making them do it, and convincing others to not give in to hardship. Sometimes all you need is for someone to reach out and with a helping hand, pull yourself up by your bootstraps."

He had a book full of Al-isms that people loved to repeat.

On education:

"You can lead a horse to water, and maybe you can't make them drink, but you can make damn sure they know why they should."

On Socialism:

"Big government is a crippling force with the best of intentions."

On corrupt politicians:

"Show me an honest politician, and I'll show you a nun who's a whore. Neither of us will have much luck."

On treating people well:

"Treat everyone the way you'd like to be treated. And if you'd like to be treated like crap, then fair enough. Do what you want."

On holiday celebrations:

"Wishing someone a Merry Christmas isn't the same as wishing someone a Crappy Hanukah. Not sure when that interpretation took hold, but it is possible to wish good things to all people. If someone wishes me a Happy Birthday when it isn't my birthday, I won't be offended. I'll stash that away for when it is."

On Hollywood stars and athletes speaking about social issues:

"I welcome all thoughts and ideas from all people. I certainly don't have all the answers. But at least I'm smart enough to know that."

and...

"When a millionaire opens their 10,000 square foot home to the homeless and goes to live in the guest house, then I'll listen to what they have to say."

On taxes:

"If Warren Buffet is so upset that he doesn't pay enough in taxes, why doesn't he ask his accountant

to not take advantage of the loopholes and send in what he thinks he should? I doubt the government would return it."

* * *

"And after not wanting to run in the first place, you ran for a second term," Gabriel laughed.

"I didn't actually run either time. The first time people started a write in campaign for me. Hell, there's only 18,000 people in the town and maybe half of them vote, so it isn't that difficult to get 5,000 votes. The second time no one ran against me."

"Because you did a good job."

"I did a job that no one else wanted to do. And it's understandable why. Name another profession where half the people hate you and you aren't getting paid millions of dollars to do it."

Gabriel nodded. He had a fair point.

Chapter 10
Goodbye

Born Brooke Carter long before she married Al Sokratis, Brooke owned a little shop in Stonington proper called a Taste of Stonington. Al thought the store name was confusing because it wasn't a restaurant and didn't actually sell anything to "taste".

"Why do you always have to be so literal?" Brooke would say to him. "The shop gives you a taste of what Stonington and Mystic are all about. The Seaport. The Beaches. The Lighthouse. The Vineyards."

"I'm a black and white person," Al would respond. "If you're going to say something is a 'taste' then you better give them something to taste."

Brooke moved from nearby Newport, Rhode Island in the early 70's when she was in her late 20's and opened the store in the heart of the borough. She had worked at a similar shop in Newport all through college and for a couple of years after it, and knew that was what she wanted to do for the rest of her life. Nearly everyone came through the store at one time or another. Locals to shop for friends and relatives that didn't live there, and vacationers as a ritual rite of passage because they wanted to actually *be* a local.

She didn't get rich owning the store, but made a decent enough living to complement Al's teaching and coaching salary, so that they could live comfortably in retirement. One day a customer came in looking for knick-knacks for her wedding reception tables and Brooke began to give suggestions on a complete nautical/vineyard theme with lighthouse and wine bottle candle holders and tables surrounding a flag pole that would double as a ship's mast. The wedding was such a hit, that Brooke soon expanded her business to include wedding and party planning.

They enjoyed a good life. Brooke attended every football game at the high school in the fall and worked the concession stand for at least two quarters. And during the summer months when Al was out of school, he'd help build any staging needed for the weddings. One time they built a makeshift boat around the tables and dance floor. Another time they used the wine barrels from one of the vineyards as tables. For one couple that wanted a casual wedding, they held it in a vineyard and all the men came in linen shirts and pants, while the women wore sundresses. All guests sported sandals and crushed grapes in their bare feet.

The plan all along had been for both to retire at the same time. Brooke would turn the store over to her young manager and she and Al would travel the country in an RV. But life had thrown them a curve ball or two which forced them to make adjustments. The first was their daughter-in-law being killed, followed closely by their son ending up in prison, which forced them to become parents for the second time. This time for their 10 year old grandson. The second curve ball came when Al was coaxed into becoming the Mayor in an election he didn't even run in. His wife supported it completely because she knew he was the best person for the job and it would be selfish of her to horde him all to herself. There would be plenty of time for that when he was done.

Four years turned into eight, before they finally were both able to retire and live the life they had imagined for themselves since the day they had met.

Al bought a 40 foot Monaco Executive RV, big and bold, with a floating living room, kitchen and two bedrooms. The plan was for them to travel across country, taking the northern route out west and returning by the southern route. He finished loading their house on wheels one early summer day and bounded up the steps of his house with the most energy he had in years.

"Let's go! The open road awaits!" he shouted.

When he didn't receive a response, he peered into the kitchen and then into the living room. Nothing. Hobbs led Al back to the bedroom where he saw his wife crumpled on the ground in an unnatural position. It took one look at her to realize she wasn't simply resting.

"She had what is called a Hemangioma of the liver. It's a benign tumor that in 98% of the people, is completely harmless. But in less than 2%, it grows until it ruptures," the doctor explained.

"Wouldn't it be easily detectable if it was that large?" Al asked.

"It would, if we were looking for it. The problem is that it rarely offers any symptoms. In Brooke's case, it grew until it burst and likely formed blood clots that stressed her heart and sent her into cardiac arrest."

"Do you think she was in any pain?"

"No. I think she probably died instantly, or very close to that. I'm very sorry, Mr. Sokratis. I wish we could have done something."

"Thanks, Doc. Thanks for trying," Al said as he shook his hand.

Sammy raced from his office before he had even listened to Al's message in its entirety. He sprinted down the hallway of the hospital and knew as soon as he saw Al seated in the waiting room with his head in his hands, that the news wasn't good.

Al shook his head. "She didn't make it."

"What happened?"

"A benign tumor burst and blood clots formed which put too much pressure on her heart."

"Jesus. I'm so sorry, G," Sammy said as he hugged his grandfather tightly.

"Thank you," Al answered before adding, "And can you stop calling me, 'G'? I'm not a rap star."

"You don't want to be called Grandpa or G Pa or Gramps because it makes you feel old," Sammy explained.

"What's wrong with simply, 'Al'?"

"I call my friends by their first name. You're much more than that."

Al nodded. "Ok. But at least call me something cool like 'Skinny G or Big G Unit or G Wheezy."

Sammy choked on his tears when he laughed. "Will do."

Al had always used humor to deflect during times of emotional stress. He hated nothing more than seeing others upset, and he knew if he wasn't able to keep it together, his grandson wouldn't either.

"I never got to say goodbye to her," Al lamented. "Never got to tell her I loved her."

"You brought her fresh flowers every single day and told her you loved her every night. Do you really think she didn't know?"

"How do you know all that?" Al asked.

"Because she told me when she was lecturing me on how to treat a woman," Sammy answered.

Al turned his head and briskly wiped away the tear that was falling down his cheek.

* * *

"Well," Gabriel said, rising slowly. Angels weren't prone to shows of emotion and Archangels even less so, but Gabriel dabbed a tear that had welled up in his own eye while watching. "I'll let you have some time to yourself."

"Thanks," Al responded quietly. "So I just need to list the five days on a sheet of paper and stick it in the mailbox?"

"That's it."

"Guess I'll see you when I see you."

"See you when I see you," Gabriel nodded. Even Archangels had their favorites.

Al paced across the floors of his home for hours after Gabriel left. When you've lived more than twenty-seven *thousand* days, choosing just five was no easy task. So many wonderful days. So many days he had regrets. So many days he wished he could go back and fix what once went wrong for others. But in the end, he could choose only five.

He scribbled the days down on a sheet of paper, stuffed it into an envelope, and placed it in the mailbox out front, leaving the flag up. He then laid down on the couch reflecting on his choices until he couldn't keep his eyes open any longer.

Chapter 11
The Cousin

Following four years as a student assistant coach in which he was a part of the National Championship staff of 1966, and two years as a grad assistant, Max Carter was named to the full-time staff as the quarterbacks coach at Notre Dame in 1969. Al Socratis was part of that national championship team as well, as the 3rd string walk on QB whose grand contribution was handing off to the 4th string running back for one play in a 64-0 blowout of Duke in the second to last game of the season.

It was the irony of ironies that the person who had never played a down of organized football in his life, was coaching at one of the most hallowed college football programs in the country, while his idol in high school, was back coaching at his high school after a stint in Vietnam. And yet, the two of them were exactly where they were always meant to be. Max was getting to exercise his creative mind and keen understanding of a game he never played. And Al was home in the town where he was a legend and would remain a legend until the day he died. Some stars were meant to give off a glow over a huge swath of people, while others were meant to illuminate only a small area and Al was at peace with that.

The two had stayed in constant touch over the years since college. Max was there the day Al returned from the war and stopped in for dinner any time he was passing through the area on a recruiting trip. They would go to Antonio's, an Italian restaurant owned by the family of one of their former classmates and sit in a booth near the front. Their dinner was nearly always interrupted five to ten times a night by people stopping to say hello, shake hands or give a pat on the back and even as Max climbed the coaching ranks and became a well-known and respected pro coach, he would never eclipse the popularity of the legend in the legend's town.

"Is it always like this for you?" Max asked.

"Is what always like this?"

"People stopping to say hello. Buying you drinks. It's a wonder you ever get to finish a meal," Max laughed.

Al shrugged. "I hadn't really noticed."

And he hadn't. He just assumed the way people treated him was the way they treated everyone, because that's how he treated everyone whose path he crossed.

"So everyone loves you, you're a good looking guy who is smart and funny, but you're still single..."

"Max. I always suspected you had an ulterior motive the day you were sniffing around the locker room," Al winked.

"I was not sniffing around!"

"I'm flattered really. But your boobs aren't big enough."

"I'm serious," Max chuckled. "How are you still single?"

"Haven't found the right one."

"What are you looking for?"

"Independent. Good sense of humor is a must. Cute but doesn't act like it."

"Soooo...Leaves you alone. Laughs at your stupid jokes. And insecure. Got it."

"That's not what I said."

"I'm just translating for you."

"Know anyone like that?"

"In fact, I do. My cousin. She lives in Rhode Island and runs a store there."

"What kind of a store?"

"Knick Knacks. Beach stuff. It's in Newport."

"Knick Knack Paddywack. Give the dog a bone. What's it called?"

"A Taste of Newport."

"Is it a restaurant?"

"Nope."

"Then what exactly are people tasting?"

"The culture of the town."

"That's just silly."

"Want to meet her?"

"What's she look like?"

"Ahh, so you are superficial after all," Max laughed.

"Look.   Everyone is. You have to be attracted to the person. The beauty is that everyone is attracted to different things. Otherwise, the two best looking people on the planet would be together and everyone else would be alone."

"I never really thought about it that way. She's a brunette. Tall. Thin. Generally considered very pretty."

"Generally?"

"I don't know. She's my cousin. I don't look at her that way. Tell you what. I'll get her to come down for the night on my way back through from Boston next Saturday. You around?"

"I think I'm going to be at Woodstock."

"You? At Woodstock?"

"Why is that so funny?"

"Well, it's all about peace, love and drugs. And you pretty much are against all three."

"I don't know. Could be kind of cool. I hear there's a lot of people headed up. I'd like to see The Who and maybe Joe Cocker and Jimi Hendrix."

"You're going to sleep outside? In the grass and dirt and mud," Max asked skeptically.

"I slept in a rice paddy field in Vietnam. I think I can handle it."

"Ok, now think of sleeping in a rice paddy field with 100,000 stoned and hallucinating strangers, who haven't showered in three days, stepping on you all night."

DAY 1–August 16, 1969

Chapter 12
Hello

"I don't know how you could sleep with all this noise and people stepping on and over you," a woman stated in Al's general direction.

It was unusual indeed for someone nicknamed the "Indian" to sleep through much of anything. It was said that he could break from a sound sleep and be fully dressed and at attention by the second note of Reveille.

Al looked up from the ground into a sea of legs and bodies everywhere. He rose slowly, pausing to take it all in—again. There were people as far as the eye could see in every direction. More than 400,000 of them to be more precise. He touched his clothes and realized he was soaking wet, although the rapidly warming August sun was doing its best impression of a heat lamp.

"It rained pretty hard last night at the end of Joan Baez's set. Plus I think some people might have spilled their drinks on you as the they walked past," she said.

One sniff of his shirt was enough to tell him she was right on all counts.

"How long was I sleeping?" he asked.

"A couple of hours I'd say. I couldn't really sleep myself."

Once the shock had worn off at having shaved 50 years off his life overnight, he more fully noticed the beautiful woman that stood before him. She was tall and thin with brown hair and deep, big, soulful brown eyes. Her flowing daffodil yellow, floral print dress ended just above mid-thigh, and showed off her long and shapely legs. She was even more beautiful than he remembered.

"I'm Brooke," she said, extending her hand.

"Nice to meet you, Brooklyn. I'm Al."

"That's not my name," she corrected.

"Everyone's name is short for something."

"And what's yours short for? Albert? Alvin?"

"Alfonze."

"Whoa. Really? Well, mine's not short for anything."

"Everybody's name is."

"Is that so?"

"Yup. Jim is short for James. Bob for Robert. Matt for Matthew. Kate for Kathleen."

"What about Kelly?"

"Kelly is the long version of Kel."

"Shawn?"

"Keyshawn."

"Keyshawn?" Brooke laughed.

"It's going to be a very popular name in a few years."

"Ok. What about Todd?" she said with a wink.

"Toddles," Al responded without hesitation.

"You've got to be joking. I have never in my life heard of anyone named 'Toddles'."

"That's because they always go by 'Todd'," Al smiled.

"So Alfonze. What do you do for a living?"

"I'm a Namer."

"I beg your pardon?"

"People come to me when they're going to have a kid and run potential names by me. My job is to point out potential difficulties for the child based on the name they choose. For example, this one couple, the Packwoods, were thinking of naming their son, Paul. But I had to rightfully point out that kids would call him 'PP' or 'Paul's Packingwood'. Neither of which would be a positive experience for their son."

Brooke was amused. "So what did you suggest?"

"No first names that began with 'P' for starters. And then to either consider changing their last name or choose a first name that wouldn't flow so easily into their last name. Something that ends in a vowel. Like George or Charlie."

"Smart," she nodded. "But that doesn't seem to be a high volume business."

"Are you kidding? People are always having babies."

"Yeah, but how much can you charge for a service like that?"

"You'd be surprised," Al winked. "Plus, some people come to me when they don't like their own name and ask me to suggest a new one for them. I have the ability to look at a person and immediately tell what name fits them. It's a gift, really."

"Is that so?"

"Take your friend here, for example. She looks like a Pete."

"Pete?? You do realize she's a female don't you?"

"Of course, but no matter. She looks sneaky. Like a Sneaky Pete. She probably used to sneak out of her bedroom window in the middle of the night back in high school to go make out with some guy at the Grove."

Brooke burst out laughing as the girl turned a crimson shade of red. "He's got you pegged!" Brooke exclaimed.

"Do we know each other?" the girl asked.

"No. We've never met. I can just tell."

"Ok. That guy over there," Brooke said, pointing to a man with long, curly hair, swim trunks and bare feet.

"Teddy."

A girl with glasses, no makeup and a dress to her ankles. "That girl."

"Becky."

"Him."

The guy had a short sleeve, button down shirt tucked into a pair of short dress shorts.

"Gordon. I can do this all day."

Brooke scanned the area before settling on a girl in a bikini top and shorts whose dancing indicated she was heavily under the influence of some kind of narcotic. A mesmerizingly slow and tantalizing movement that you couldn't look away from.

"Jade."

"You're good," Brooke agreed at last. "Man, I would kill for a pretzel. The lines for food are outrageous and word has it they're almost out."

"Well, it just so happens that I can help you with that," Al said, reaching into his backpack. He pulled out a bag of pretzels and handed them over. Brooke devoured them like a coyote that hadn't eaten in weeks.

"Thank you," she said between bites. "Anything else fun in that bag?"

"A few cans of Chef Boyardee and some Pop Tarts."

"Are you a Boy Scout or an Astronaut?" she asked.

"Neither. Was a solider."

"And   you're here?" she   laughed.   "That rules us out."

"Out of what?"

"Dating."

"I didn't know we were," Al smiled.

"I can't date an Army guy."

"Well, I was only in for two and a half weeks if that counts for anything."

"Did you run away?" she asked, intrigued.

"Sort of."

"Are   you   AWOL?"   she   followed, increasingly excited.

"No," Al chuckled. "I got shot, and they sent me home."

"You got shot? Where?"

"My back," he answered.

"Never   known   anyone   who   got   shot before."

"Now you have."

"How do I know you're telling the truth?"

He lifted his shirt to show her the bullet wound.

"Coooool. So what percentage of the things you've told me today are actually true?" she asked.

"I'd say roughly five percent," Al said.

"That's higher than I would have guessed."

"Well, I did get shot."

"So what are you doing here, solider boy?"

"Just came to listen to some music with some teacher friends of mine from Connecticut."

"You're a teacher?"

"Yes, ma'am."

"And you're from Connecticut?"

"Yes, ma'am."

"I'm from Rhode Island."

"And what do you do in Rhode Island?" Al asked, eager to shift the conversation away.

"I run a store in Newport."

"What kind of store?"

"A knick knack store."

"It's not called A Taste of Newport by any chance is it? Even though there's nothing to taste?"

"How did you know that?"

"Your last name Carter?" Al asked.

"It is, but if you tell me I just look like a Carter, I'm going to slap you."

"You're Max's cousin."

"Al Socrates?"

"So-krat-is."

"He's been trying to set me up with you for ages!"

"He's a smart man."

"Jury's out on that." And then, "The bands aren't supposed to start back up for a while. You want to go for a walk?"

"How will we find our way back in this

madness?"

"If we don't, at least we'll have each other," she smiled as she grabbed his hand and led him away.

* * *

They spent the next few hours in each other's company. Drinking with strangers. Taking a bath in the nearby pond, where they came out just as dirty as when they went in. Making out in a meadow. And of course listening to music. Some great, some Al could have done without.

Quill opened the day with a short set, followed by *Country Joe McDonald* and *Santana*. In the evening, *The Grateful Dead* played along with *Creedence Clearwater Revival*. It was late at night or early in the morning at that point depending on your perspective and with some people having barely slept in more than 24 hours, the crowd had quieted down as many took the opportunity to rest. Others had drifted off long before that, succumbing to the various hallucinogenics they had ingested.

"You know, it could rain again tonight," Al hinted.

"And it could get cold," Brooke answered.

"I have a sleeping bag. And you have a tent. Should we pool our resources?" he asked hopefully, but without much hope.

"You mean sleep together? I don't know. That sounds a bit forward. I just met you."

"Not necessarily sleep together, but sleep next to each other. That way we could both be warm and dry."

"I'm just teasin. Get your ass over here with your sleeping bag. I was going to steal it anyway," she laughed.

Even though he knew her answer would be yes, Al was inside her tent within seconds. He wasn't giving her the opportunity to change her mind. She zipped the tent closed for some privacy among the hundreds of thousands of people and crawled inside the bag. Al joined her and zipped the bag tight around them both.

"Now I'm hot," Al said. "I think I'm going to need to take off my shorts."

"If you must. But make sure you stay on your side of the bag. No touching."

"That might be a bit difficult," he answered as he tucked his arm underneath hers. She clenched her arm tight around it, and it was quite possibly the greatest feeling he had ever had.

When *The Who* finally took the stage at nearly 5:00am, Brooke had long been asleep. Eventually, Al's eyes began to close and his head nod, but he fought it with every ounce of energy in his body because he knew once he closed his eyes, his very best day would be over and a three hour nap would become fifteen years. *See Me, Feel Me* was the last song he remembered hearing and he clung to his soon to be wife tightly as if doing so would prevent the day from ending.

"There had better be a thermos inside this bag," she mumbled, half asleep.

Chapter 13
A Charmed Life

Al never applied for the Teacher in Space Program, so imagine his surprise when he received a call saying he was one of the two nominees from the great state of Connecticut. One of his colleagues had applied for him.

Even then, Al never seriously thought he had a chance of being selected to go on a space shuttle mission with actual astronauts. An objective view would see things differently. He was a math teacher and the program's stated mission was to expand interest in math and science to a host of young people. He was an athlete, which would make him much more likely to pass the fitness tests and requirements of the program. And he was a war hero, which would play well with the press when it came time to publicize the program. So it was a surprise to no one but Al, when he was chosen as one of the 10 national finalists for the position.

And yet even though he never applied for the position and never thought he had a serious chance of being selected, he was devastated when he was chosen as the backup, to a bright and effervescent high school Social Studies teacher from New Hampshire that they thought would play better than the sometimes dour and always measured Al. He never let on to his disappointment, however, and dutifully trained as the understudy for a role he would never get to play, for more than a year with the crew that would eventually go up in the Challenger Space Shuttle.

The day before the launch, Al boarded a plane in Orlando and flew back into Tweed Airport in New Haven, Connecticut, where he returned to his family and the only job he had ever known. He was watching in the school auditorium with the entire student body and most of his friends and family that afternoon, when the Challenger exploded 73 seconds into its flight. Al was overcome by equally strong emotions; a feeling of gut-wrenching sadness at losing his friends on the shuttle that had become like family to him, along with the eerie voice of his mother telling him that "everything happens for a reason", which left him feeling obligated to live the best life he could from that moment on. He also made sure to hold his wife a little tighter that night.

DAY 2 — January 26, 1986

Chapter 14
The Understudy

The alarm clock in Al's hotel room switched from 5:46 to 5:47am and started buzzing like it was its job—which it was. It was really only 5:33, but Al always set his clocks ahead 14 minutes, so that his alarm would always go off at either 17 or 47 minutes after the hour, in part because 17 and 47 were his two favorite numbers, but mainly because he thought it helped him always be on time while creating the illusion that he was getting more sleep.

It took him a moment to gather his bearings. He had gone to sleep hugging his soon to be wife inside a tent at Woodstock in 1969, and woke up alone in a hotel room in Cape Canaveral, Florida seventeen years later.

At 6:15, NASA sent a car to drive him the three miles to the Kennedy Space Center.

"You leaving us today, Al?" a security guard inside the front entrance asked.

"Yessir, Shawno. Just came to say my goodbyes," Al answered.

"We're going to miss you around here," Shawn said as he pulled him in for a bear hug. "You better come back and visit us."

"I definitely will. You take care of yourself. And the wife. And the little ones."

The six astronauts and the teacher that would be joining them had been in quarantine with the backup crew for just under a week in order to minimize the risk of illness during the mission. Vomit would not be an easy cleanup in a weightlessness environment.

Ten days before the flight, they all underwent a physical called the L-10, standing for ten days before the launch physical. Two days before the flight, they underwent another one, at which point the backup crew was released if everyone on the main crew was deemed healthy. Contact with the outside world was limited after that to an isolation room with a thick glass partition not unlike what you might find in a prison or bank lobby.

Dick Scobee was selected as the Commander of the Challenger following a successful mission two years earlier to deploy one satellite and repair another. He was a Lieutenant Colonel in the Air Force, who had served as a Combat Aviator in Vietnam. Al and Dick were roughly the same age. They both had played football in high school, and both began their careers in the military as enlisted men who served in Vietnam at the same time – Al serving on the ground in Minh Thanh, while Dick flew over it in a Caribou cargo jet. But while Al was the person for whom success usually came easily, Dick Scobee had to work hard at it, whether it be in the classroom, football field, or in flight school. They had lived parallel lives, growing up on opposite coasts of the country from each other. And they were kindred spirits, both devoted husbands and fathers, who shied away from the spotlight until it inevitably found them. Dick had taken a liking to Al immediately and the bond only grew in the months that followed.

"Homeward bound?" Dick asked as he made his way to the partition to greet Al.

"Yep. Thought it was about time I stopped playing astronaut and rejoined my real life. They're taking me by chopper to Orlando Airport in about an hour or so."

"Wish you were going with us."

"I appreciate that and I appreciate everything you did to make me feel welcome here for the past several months. It was an experience I will never forget."

"If this program goes well, maybe you'll get to be on the next mission."

"About the mission," Al began slowly, "Are you concerned at all about launching in these temperatures?"

"They're telling us it will be fine."

"Didn't one of the directors of Morton Thiokol refuse to sign off on launching below a certain temperature?"

"I think that's been the reason for the delays, but they've assured us we are going up tomorrow. Might be in the afternoon though."

"Here's the thing that I worry about. The O Rings that seal the solid rocket boosters are made of rubber. When it's warm, rubber expands and molds. When it's frozen, it snaps. And somewhere in between the two, I wonder whether it will — "

" — seal properly," Dick finished his sentence for him.

"Exactly. And if the flames escape the rocket..."

"...it will explode. I get it. But people a lot smarter than us don't seem too concerned."

"But why not wait a few more days for the temperature to go back up? What would be the harm in that?"

"Probably none, but I don't think they're going to wait any longer."

"Tell them to wait. You're the Commander. They'll listen to you," Al urged.

"They'll replace me is what they'll do," Dick laughed.

Al nodded. "To safe launches and smooth landings," he said, pressing his hand against the glass as a high five.

"Safe launches and smooth landings," Dick repeated.

Al wasn't going to give up that easily. He managed to bulldoze his way into a conference room where several of the important decision makers were meeting, under the guise of thanking them and saying goodbye.

"We've enjoyed having you here, Al," one of them said. "Keep in touch. Hope your football team wins State next fall."

"Thank you. But before I go, there's something I have to say or I couldn't live with myself. Maybe it was all part of some crazy dream I had, but it seemed very real and it got me thinking."

"About what?"

"About the O Rings."

"What about them?" one of the other men interjected.

"They're made of rubber. Hard rubber, but rubber nonetheless."

"And your point is?"

"When it's hot, rubber melds and molds. It seals. When it's frozen, it could snap. And when it's cold, it might not snap, but it certainly won't mold and seal."

"I thought you were an Algebra teacher?"

"Math and Science. Do you have a freezer

nearby?" Al asked as he grabbed two empty glasses on the table. "I also need a blow torch."

"Excuse me?"

"Guys. It's a rocket command center. I'm sure you've got a blow torch around here somewhere."

The man in charge shook his head and rolled his eyes, but motioned to someone else to go get one. That had to signify a glimmer of hope, because there was no way they would have entertained the folly of a high school teacher if they weren't having some doubts of their own.

Al removed two large, thick rubber bands from his pocket. He handed one over to the guard who was escorting him through the building. "Pete, can you pop this in the freezer for a bit?"

When the other man returned with a small blow torch, Al took one of the glasses and placed the rubber band around the rim of the open end. Everyone jumped back when he fired up the torch without warning and began to heat the rubber band. It melted around the edge. He then flipped the other glass face down on top of the band and pressed them together. It sealed tightly.

Turning to Pete he asked, "Can you hold these two glasses together sideways for me?"

Al grabbed a glass of half full water from

one of the men and poured it onto the seal between the two glasses. Not a drop went inside.

He raised his palms as if he expected applause and a Nobel Prize, but neither came.

"It's sealed," Al said.

"Congratulations," the first man responded.

"Pete. Can you grab that rubber band from the freezer?" Al asked.

A few uncomfortable minutes later, Pete returned with it.

"It's not frozen," Al said, holding it up for a visual. "But it's showing cracks and it's hard as a rock."

He grabbed two more empty glasses and placed the rubber band on the open-faced glass before once again pressing the other one on top of it. This time, the rubber cracked and there were gaps between the two glasses. Al turned to Pete once again for his help. He felt like a magician about to saw his assistant in half. This time when he poured the water, it went everywhere. On the table yes, but also inside both glasses, even with Pete holding them tightly together.

"Look. I know this was a crude demonstration. And I know I'm not a rocket scientist. But the point remains the same. The glasses didn't seal with a very pliable rubber band. Now picture a very hard piece of nearly frozen rubber and a solid rocket with explosive gasses and flames escaping."

Five minutes passed and no one in the room said a word.

As Al sat on the three hour flight home, he couldn't escape the thought that not only had he not made a single difference in the outcome of the lives of his seven friends, but he had wasted one of his gifted five days. But then he saw his wife waiting at the gate as he exited the plane and the all-enveloping hug he received from her reassured him that it had definitely been worthwhile after all.

Chapter 15
Into the Darkness

Ever since he could remember, Rich Cosgrove felt as though his life was cursed. There wasn't any one thing that made him feel that way, but rather a host of them. Life would cruise along just fine, until a big moment would come along, and it would *never* work out in his favor.

Down to the last spot to make the varsity football team in high school, he sprained his ankle and was unable to finish the tryout. He had a shot with the cutest girl in the high school until the captain of the basketball team slid in at the last minute and took her to the Homecoming Dance. Only to dump her two weeks later. Needing a certain SAT score on his last try to be admitted to the only school he and his family could afford, his car broke down on the way to the test and he missed it. He was a die hard Red Sox fan who watched them narrowly miss out on winning a World Series twice, if you don't also count 1946 when he was three. In 1967 and 1975, he watched the Sox win Game 6, only to lose the decisive Game 7 both times.

So it came as no surprise to Rich that when Lyndon Johnson increased the numbers of the men drafted into Vietnam, he was one of the first ones drafted. He actually never feared dying in the war. His fear was *not* dying, but living in pain and agony for the rest of his life. And when Al dragged him to safety on that fateful day in 1966, that's exactly what happened.

He lost his left leg below the knee in surgery while in Vietnam and his return to U.S. soil was bittersweet. He was alive, but with severely wounded pride, unable to walk without crutches and viewed as a spectacle to all who saw him. At least that's how he saw it in his mind.

Eventually, he received a prosthetic leg, which enabled him to walk, but with a severe limp that he was so self-conscious of, he never wore shorts again, no matter how warm it was outside. He also withdrew from his friends, his job as the manager at a supermarket, and eventually, from life itself.

Al tried repeatedly to draw him back out, but even he gave up after a while.

"I wish you had left me to die over there," Rich told him once.

"You don't mean that."

"I do. I'm a circus act. A clown without the laughter."

"You are the same person you always were. You just walk a little slower."

"My life is over."

"What would make you happy? Let's focus on that."

"The Red Sox winning the World Series."

"Ehhhh," Al hesitated. "Can you give me something a little easier to work with?"

"Ok. Who is going to love me?"

"A lot of people love you, me included."

"I meant a female."

"In order for others to love you, you have to first love yourself."

"I can't even wear shorts or walk normally without people staring."

"Who cares?" Al shot back. "Where is the person who never cared what anyone else thought? The person who would be the first to defend those that needed it."

"I couldn't defend a church mouse now."

"You never defended them with your fists or your legs. You defended them with your wit, your charm, your caring. That's what people loved about you then and what they still love about you now."

But try though he might, he couldn't get through, and one night, on his 42nd birthday, Rich took his .45 caliber pistol from the war, cleaned it, loaded it, and fired a single bullet into his skull.

Six months later, the Red Sox blew leads in both Games 6 and 7 of the World Series and lost to the Mets.

DAY 3 — April 17, 1986

Chapter 16
Rich Cosgrove's Day Off

Al knocked on the apartment door with enough authority that it echoed throughout the hallway. The brick building wasn't dilapidated, but it was in desperate need of a face lift. After some shuffling inside, Rich opened the door.

"Al? What are you doing here?" Rich seemed surprised, and maybe a little irritated.

"What's up, my man? I'm here to take you on a day off."

"I've got to work," Rich answered briskly.

"You've already called in sick."

"How do you know that?"

"Don't worry how I know. I just know. Besides, if you were going to work, you'd already be there," Al reasoned.

When Rich didn't answer, Al knew it to be true.

"Today, I am Ferris Bueller to your Cameron. But instead of going to see the Cubs, we're headed to Fenway Park," Al said, holding up two box seats as proof.

"Where'd you get those?" Rich asked.

"Don't worry about where I got 'em. Worry

about having a shave, shower, and if necessary, a shit, so we can get some breakfast before heading to Boston."

"I'll have two scrambled eggs with melted cheese over them, sausage patties, hash browns and white toast, with a side of corn beef hash and a short stack of pancakes," Al told the waitress at the local diner. When he noticed the incredulous look on Rich's face, he added, "What?"

"Are you serious with that order?" Rich asked. "Why don't you just order a heart attack on a plate?"

"I could get hit by a car tomorrow and I don't want my last meal to be cream of wheat and a banana."

Rich turned to the waitress and shrugged, "Same."

"So how are things?" Al asked.

"Every day, I get up at 5:30am, so I can be at the store by 6:30, at which point I undoubtedly find out that someone has called in sick. I then spend the next hour trying to find coverage on short notice and when I can't, I end up stocking shelves for three hours until I get a call that the next delivery truck is going to be late. Two hours and twenty phone calls later, I get word that they won't be in until 2:00am so I've got to come back in to greet them and sign off. But before that happens, I have to get screamed at by customers unhappy with our produce, meats or service. If I'm lucky, I get to go home at 7:00pm, eat a TV dinner and fall asleep in my lounge chair watching the Sox game. Lather. Rinse. Repeat."

"Your day doesn't sound much different than mine. I'm up at 6:00am so I can be at school for 7:00. I teach high school Algebra and Trig for the first two periods, which puts even the most energetic kids to sleep, and at that hour, you can actually hear the snoring coming from the classroom out in the hallway. By 11:00, when the real world has just finished breakfast and a coffee, I'm eating lunch in the faculty lounge because I've already been up for five hours, where I have to listen to other teachers complain that I have a cream puff schedule because I coach football. Meanwhile, I didn't see any of them at the game until 10:30pm Friday night cleaning up and watching game film for a grand total of thirty-two cents per hour. On a good day, I get home from practice at 6:30, followed by grading a stack of papers until I fall asleep watching the Mets instead of the Red Sox."

"But at least you get to do that with a family."

"You could do that too," Al reasoned.

Rich paused for a moment, not sure exactly

how to phrase his response. "Look, I'm grateful that you risked your own life to save mine, I really am. But some days, most days actually, I wish you had left me to die in that rice paddy field in Vietnam."

"You don't mean that," Al answered.

"Sadly, I do."

"Look, there are two certainties in this world. Life is full of disappointments. But that's what makes you appreciate the good days that much more. When I wasn't selected to go up in the space shuttle, I was devastated. But then I came home and saw my family and friends and realized that was the only place I wanted to be."

"Probably rethinking that a bit now that she's set to be a millionaire," Rich remarked.

"I beg your pardon?"

"She's writing a book on the trip and they're making a movie."

"On the shuttle exploding?"

"What are you talking about? It didn't explode. We watched it together in the high school auditorium three and a half months ago."

"No shit," Al smiled.

"Have you been drinking?"

"Only orange juice. So they all lived?"

"Uh, yeah. They've only been on TV every day since they returned."

"That's incredible news."

"You've lost it, my friend. So what's the second certainty in life? Unless you forgot that too?"

"Of course not. The second certainty is that you'll never find that special someone in your apartment. You've got to get out and do things you enjoy. That way when you run into someone, you'll know you share a common interest."

"That would be great if I wanted to marry a loud mouthed, fat, drunken Sox fan."

"People have done worse," Al laughed. "So tell me, until you find that special person to share your life with, if I could grant you one other wish, what would it be?"

"That the Sox will win the World Series."

"Jesus, man. Do you want me to walk on water too? They haven't won the Series in 68 years. Can't we start with something a little easier—like winning the lottery?"

"You asked what I wanted."

"Fine. It's done."

"Oh really?" Rich laughed, amused.

"Yup. Now you've got something to look forward to."

The Red Sox beat the Royals that day, 6-2, before 10,583 fans at Fenway Park. Roger Clemens threw a complete game for the win, and Rich caught a foul ball in their seats behind the Red Sox dugout. It wasn't an accident.

The night Al chose his five days, he watched the game in its entirety, including where every foul ball landed. When he found one that landed in empty seats, he bought tickets to the game as close to that spot as he could.

Following the game, Al told an usher that Rich was a Vietnam War hero, and they soon found themselves escorted to the Sox locker room to meet the team. They were all there changing. Clemens. Jim Rice. Dwight Evans. Wade Boggs. Don Baylor. Bill Buckner. While Rich went straight for Boggs and Clemens, Al sought out Buckner, who was alone on a stool in front of his locker.

"Hi Bill. I've been a fan of yours for a long time. Going back to your days as a Dodger."

"Thank you very much," Buckner responded. "I appreciate that."

"I have to ask you, as someone who almost never strikes out, how do you adjust from batting against a pitcher who throws smoke to a guy who throws slow, but with a three foot break on his curve? It has to be really tough."

"Hitting is all about timing and out thinking the pitcher. Once you get the timing down, you'll know when to start your swing. When going from a fast pitcher to a slow one with a lot of breaking stuff, your first instinct is usually to take a couple of pitches to get your timing down. But then the pitcher will think you'll do that and groove a couple to get ahead in the count. So what I do instead is swing at the first pitch because he's going to assume I won't."

"Sounds like a chess match."

"That's exactly what it is," he nodded.

"So this is going to sound really weird," Al began slowly, uncertain how to say what he felt he needed to say, "but in six months, when you're playing in the World Series against the Mets..."

"We're going to make the World Series? I like your optimism."

"You are. And when you find yourself up 3 games to 2 and up 5-4 in game 6, with Bob Stanley on the mound, Kevin Mitchell at 3rd with Ray Knight at 1st and Mookie Wilson at the plate, I need you to do me a favor."

"Wow. That's a pretty specific dream you had," Buckner laughed.

"Except it wasn't a dream."

"You a psychic?"

"Kind of."

"Interesting. Know tonight's lottery numbers by any chance?"

"3. 11. 17. 20. 33."

He said it with such conviction, even Buckner had to take pause for a moment.

"Look. I know you don't believe me now, and I don't blame you, but when all this happens, you need to tell Gedman he needs to slide to his right and block Stanley's wild pitch on the 7th pitch of the at bat. Three pitches later, you need to guard the line and cheat forward. That way, when Mookie hits a slow roller up the first base line, you'll catch it early. And most importantly, make sure you keep your glove down."

"I promise," an amused Buckner nodded. "You must be a real die hard Sox fan."

"To be honest, I'm actually a Mets fan, but he's a die hard Sox fan," Al said, pointing at Rich across the locker room laughing with Boggs. "And I'd do anything for him. Plus, I've always liked you. I want people to remember you for the incredible career you had and not just one play."

"Boy, I must have really screwed the pooch, huh?"

"Not this time you won't," Al assured him.

Chapter 17
The Sixth Sense

The last thing Al did just before the kickoff of every game was to look in the stands for his wife, son and grandson. Seeing them reassured him that everything was going to be all right, no matter the outcome of the game. When they were caught in traffic one night and didn't make kickoff, he was all out of sorts until they arrived.

Then one night, he looked into the stands and saw his wife and grandson, but there was no sign of his son. Jimmy could have been in the restroom or at the concession stand, but after looking up 8 or 9 times to the point where players had begun asking him what he was looking at, he came to the conclusion Jimmy simply wasn't there.

At the final whistle, Al was approached by one of the off duty officers that was working security at the game.

"There's a problem with Jimmy," the guard whispered.

"What do you mean, 'problem'?"

"I probably shouldn't be telling you this

because they haven't released any of the details yet, but Jimmy was involved in a struggle with the owner of the mini mart on the other side of town. There was a gun. Not sure whose it was. The owner was killed in the struggle. That's all I know. Jimmy's at the station. But you didn't hear anything from me."

Other than burying a child, the next worst feeling for a parent had to be seeing one of their children locked up in a holding cell. Whether it was for a DUI, a fight, drugs or worse made no difference. Seeing his first and only child behind bars, was a memory Al would never be able to shake.

They wouldn't let him see Jimmy for nearly eight hours, until he had slept it off. He looked like a version of death warmed over.

"What the hell happened?" were the first words Al spoke to him.

"The guy pulled a gun on me so I pulled him over the counter and wrestled him to the ground. In the struggle, the gun went off," Jimmy answered.

"Why were you so drunk? What were you doing on that side of town? And why would he pull a gun on you?"

"Because he thought I had one."

"And why would he think that?"

"Because I pretended I did."

"What were you thinking?!" Al demanded

to know.

"I wasn't, dad. But I was desperate. I've been working three jobs. I'm exhausted all the time. And I still don't have any money."

"If it's money you needed, I'd have helped you. You know that."

"That's the point. You and mom have done enough. You watch Sammy for me all the time. You've given me plenty of money. At some point, I need to be able to make it on my own."

"And you think stealing from someone else is making it on your own?"

"For Sammy's birthday last week, I got him this shitty little plastic nerf hoop because it was all I could afford. And he smiled and hugged me like I had given him a car, and it made me feel even worse."

"That's because to him, the only thing that matters is that you remembered and gave him something. It's all he's talked about for two days. Sammy doesn't need a car. He needs to know his dad cares about him. And that's enough."

Tears starting pouring down Jimmy's face and the sight of his thirty-two year old son sobbing, was enough to bring his grizzled war veteran father with a heart of gold to tears for the first time in 50 years.

Day 4 — October 17, 2003

Chapter 18
Making a Bad Day, Good

Being around someone every day often caused you to miss any changes in their appearance. Not being around them for a decade caused you to forget even the simplest and most beautiful of things, like their smile and the peaceful way they slept. Al began most days by doing what he referred to as "performing his ablutions", but on this day, that could wait.

After ten years, he had almost forgotten what his wife looked like in detail. Pictures didn't do her justice, and he was determined to spend all morning if he needed to, memorizing every turn of her lips, the wrinkle of her nose, the sparkle in her blue eyes.

It was the simple things he missed most about her. Things like the lilt of her voice any time she got excited and her high-pitched giggle whenever she was shocked by something. He loved those things about her so much that he would often find himself saying shocking things just to hear her reaction.

The toast was slightly burnt, but the scrambled eggs were scrambled to perfection, and the small bowl of oatmeal smelled amazing with cinnamon and brown sugar topping it. He carried it into the bedroom on a tray and woke up his wife with a gentle kiss on the cheek.

"What's this?" she asked sleepily, rubbing her eyes like a five year old after a nap. Even at 60, she had never lost her youthful mannerisms. "It's not my birthday."

"No, it's not," Al responded.

"So you need a favor..." she smiled as she propped herself up and took the tray on her lap.

"Can't a guy make breakfast in bed for his wife without needing something?"

"Experience tells me otherwise."

"I just missed you is all."

"Since yesterday?" she asked curiously.

"Yes. I didn't get to see you much. Is that so awful?"

"Of course not. It's just not like you to be..."

"To be?"

"Nice?"

"I think I'm going to take my eggs and oatmeal back."

"I don't mean that in a bad way."

"Yes, because there's so many *good* ways to take that," Al laughed.

"It's just unusual," Brooke responded. "You're usually my lovable curmudgeon."

"I'm pacing myself with good deeds."

She giggled her surprised giggle and Al knew he was home again.

***

The students began to stagger into Al's homeroom five minutes before the second bell sounded, signaling the official start to the school day. He nodded in acknowledgment and greeted each and every one of them as they passed his desk. As the morning announcements began, he logged into his computer and Googled "Challenger Space Shuttle". The results stunned him.

"Delayed three weeks over concerns about the cold temperatures at launch, along with internal fighting over the effectiveness of the 'O Ring' seals for the rocket boosters, the Challenger Space Shuttle was launched on February 11, 1986, the first to carry a civilian teacher into space, as part of Ronald Reagan's Teacher in Space Program. The mission was declared a complete success when Christa McCauliffe taught multiple science lessons to the nation's children from outer space. Unfortunately, the same concerns that had delayed the original Challenger launch, were proven well-founded when a subsequent mission ended in an explosion shortly after take off. All 7 members of that crew, which included 2 members of the original crew died in the

tragedy."

Al's face turned ashen. He had saved the lives of five of his friends, but cost the lives of five strangers. He didn't feel nearly qualified enough to be making those types of decisions, the very thought of which consumed him for the rest of the day. And yet, he still needed to push onward in his effort to save another life.

Al thought it was simply amazing the way time had the ability to turn even the most mundane of tasks and turn them into cherished memories. Years ago when he was teaching, he dreaded homeroom, trying to take attendance while kids wandered in late with a host of excuses as to why they were, jabbering on about their weekend festivities that Al did not want to know about. When they would try to involve him in their conversations, he would pretend he didn't hear them, make a fake phone call, even feign sleep if necessary. Sixteen years later, he realized just how much he had missed it all. Students including him in their lives wasn't a nuisance. It was an honor, especially when you considered how rarely they wanted to share much of anything with an adult.

"Mr. S. You missed a great party at Ronnie's this weekend. It was slammin. His family has a vineyard in their backyard!" Tom Evans shouted.

"Sorry I missed it," Al laughed, "but I'm guessing it was more fun without me."

"Heck no. We could have shot-gunned beer together."

"He doesn't know what shot-gunning a beer is, stupido," Pete Jones chimed in.

"Do you guys seriously think you invented the shotgun? I was doing those for two decades before your parents even met."

"Tell 'em how it is, Mr. S!" Tom said.

"Of course my shot-gunning days are far behind me," Al added. "And yours should be too. You're not of age."

"Were you of age when you did it?"

"Actually yes. The drinking age was 18 when I was growing up."

"No kidding. That's really cool."

"Yeah, but then they decided teenagers weren't mature enough to handle it," Al winked. "Besides, too much of anything will cause problems later in life. Trust me on that. Acid reflux. Stomach issues. Definitely not worth it."

"Ok, ok," Tom began. "Serious question unrelated to alcohol."

"I can hardly contain myself from the excitement."

"Do you think it would be poor form if Pete took a shot at Ronnie's ex-girlfriend?"

"I think that would definitely be considered

poor form, yes."

"Ronnie knows about it, and he's ok with it I should add."

"Women are not property, like a car, where you can just sign over the title. Does this girl know of his plans?"

"Of course she does. She likes him."

"Are they dating?" Al asked.

"People don't date anymore, Mr. S. But they're talking if that's what you mean."

"You and I are talking."

"That's a different kind of talking," Tom laughed.

"I don't know, Tom. Out of the literally hundreds of thousands of people I've known in my life, I've known about five that married their high school sweethearts. Only two of them are still together."

"No one said anything about marrying her," Tom responded.

"But that's my point. Since they're not going to get married, does he really need to 'take a shot' at a girl his friend dated? He might say he's ok with it, but is he really? And is it worth potentially ruining a friendship over?"

"It could be," Tom smiled.

"Abstinence makes the heart grow fonder."

"Isn't it *absence* makes the heart grow fonder?" Pete asked.

"Is it?" Al asked with a knowing smile.

"No offense, but that sounds really hard, Mr. S."

"It's supposed to be hard. If it wasn't hard, everyone would do it. It's the hard that makes it great."

"That's pretty profound."

"It is.   But I can't take credit for it. I borrowed it from *A League of their Own*."

"Thought it sounded familiar."

"Look. You guys have to learn to treat woman with respect. Even if they don't respect themselves."

"What makes you think she doesn't respect herself?" Tom asked.

"She dated Ronnie and is considering being with Pete, isn't she?"

"That's   ice   cold,   Mr.   S," Pete answered. "*Ice* cold."

The bell rang and going against the flow of students trying to exit the classroom, Rich Cosgrove entered.

"Lunch in the faculty lounge?" he asked.

A stunned Al nodded, "Definitely."

***

The first half of the game that night went exactly as he remembered it. They played decently, but missed a late field goal and went into halftime tied at 10.

Al grabbed Joe Benedetto in the locker room. "I've got to go."

"You've got to what?"

"I've got to go. Family emergency."

"Everything ok?"

"It's Jimmy. I'll explain later. Here," Al said, thrusting a piece of paper into Joe's hand.

"What's this?"

"The play script for the second half."

"You scripted the entire half?" Joe asked incredulously.

"Stick to it. Especially the last series. On the final play, they're going to pretend to stack the box, but then drop into coverage to stop the fade routes. Have Lance run a QB Draw. He'll moonwalk into the end zone."

"I don't understand. How do you know what they're going to do?"

"Don't worry about how I know. I just know," Al responded before adding, "I watched a lot of film."

Al arrived at the gas station across town at 9:15. He remembered the police report saying the incident took place at 9:32. Now he just had to wait. His son pulled in shortly thereafter, got out of his car and hesitated briefly, before heading for the door.

"Don't do it, Jimmy," Al stated plainly.

The recognition of the familiar voice startled him. Jimmy spun around. "Dad? What are you doing here?"

"When I didn't see you at the game, I came looking for you."

"But how did you find me?" Jimmy demanded to know.

"Don't worry about that. The more important question is what you're doing here to begin with?"

"I'm just going to get a snack."

"You could have done that much closer to home."

"I felt like going for a drive."

"As drunk as you are, you shouldn't be driving anywhere."

"Have you been following me?"

"No, I've been coaching. I had a game tonight. That you were supposed to be at with your son."

"I had a bad day."

"I understand. And I want to hear all about it over a beer. But you're going to leave your car here and ride with me. We'll get your car in the morning."

Jimmy stared at his father. Even at 60, he was athletic and tough. You didn't want to mess with him. He nodded his head, and climbed into the passenger seat of Al's truck.

They bellied up to the bar at a local establishment where you might have been wise to wipe around the edge of your glass with a napkin before drinking from it.

"Talk to me," Al said.

"I've been working three jobs. I'm exhausted all the time. And I still can't pay my bills, much less save anything. I used to be the man. Star athlete. Got all the women. Now I feel like a loser."

"You're hardly a loser. You played professional hockey. Married a beautiful, sweet woman and had an amazing kid. Those things alone, put you in the top 2% of the population. But you've hit a rough patch. You lost your wife in a tragic accident that you had nothing to do with. You're done playing hockey, and now you've got to reinvent yourself. But the good news is you can."

"How am I going to do that? I don't even have a degree."

"Then get your degree. They have these online courses now. You can take them whenever you have time."

"And how am I going to pay for them?"

"I'll pay for them, and before you start in with 'I've done enough', let me remind you that I was always planning to help you pay for college. I'm just doing it a little bit later is all. In the meantime, I've talked to the AD at Stonington, and they're looking for a new hockey coach. You could take over the house that you built. How cool would that be?"

When Jimmy didn't answer, he knew he had him thinking. It was as close to agreeing with him as he was going to get.

"Life isn't always easy, but it can be amazing. It's just tough to see that sometimes. By the way, that nerf hoop you gave Sammy for his birthday? It's all he talks about. Pretending to be Dr. Dunkenstein. Chocolate Thunder. His Airness. He can't make a free throw in a real game, but he can dunk the hell out of a nerf ball," Al chuckled.

"It was just a stupid little gift."

"You don't get it. It doesn't matter what you give him. He's going to love it, because it's from you. You've got it easy. You've got such a great kid, that you don't need to be rich. Or cool. You just need to be there. And you can't very well be there if you're in jail."

"Understood," Jimmy whispered.

***

After saying goodnight to his son and leaving him in the guest room to sleep it off, Al sat down at the desk in his home office and turned on his computer. He wasn't what one would call computer savvy, but was capable of searching the internet when needed. In the excitement of the day, he never had a chance to research something that had been on his mind the moment Rich Cosgrove stuck his head into his classroom.

He googled *"1986 World Series"*. But instead of a picture of Ray Knight rounding 3rd base and heading home, he found a picture of Bill Buckner, All Star and former National League batting champion, hoisting the Commissioner's Trophy high over his head for the World Series champion, Boston Red Sox. Al nodded and smiled as pulled on a New York Mets t-shirt and climbed into bed.

Chapter 19
The Best Man

Sammy Sokratis couldn't sleep. His mind was racing over a combination of excitement and fear. Excitement at the hope that his girlfriend of two years was about to become his finance. And fear for the exact same reason. Sure, there was a small part of him that was concerned she might say "no", but when you had spent as much time together as they had, and knew each other as well as they did, as long you went into it with clear eyes, you had to be pretty certain the direction it would go before you asked.

But there was a big difference between dating someone and living with them. Between living with them and being married to them. When you were dating, you always saw each other at your best. Cleaned up to go out. Didn't have to deal with the clutter of a shared bathroom. But as his grandfather always told him, "You know when you know, and no amount of logic to the contrary should ever get in your way."

Armed with that piece of advice from the

man who had been equal parts father and grandfather to him, Sammy dropped to one knee as they sat on a bench looking out into the Atlantic Ocean during one of their morning walks.

"Did you lose a contact?" his girlfriend asked innocently.

"I'm not very good with things like this," he began.

"Things like what?" She really didn't have a clue.

"We've been together now for nearly two years," he said. "And sure, we've had our ups and downs like any couple, but the difference is that our worst of times has still been better than the best I've ever experienced with anyone else."

The teardrop that was slowly falling over her cheekbone indicated she finally understood where he was headed with this.

"I know it won't be perfect. And I know I'm not perfect. But I'm hoping you would consider being imperfect together. As my grandfather says, 'You know when you know'. And I know I want you as my wife—if you'll have me."

Full fledged waterworks were flowing now. She didn't even look at the ring he held out before her, choosing instead to throw her arms around him with an emphatic "YES" for an answer.

Following several excited calls to her parents and her sisters to tell them the news, there was only one person Sammy wanted to speak to. And he wanted to do it in person, so he hopped in his car and made the ten minute drive across town to the old southern colonial with the white picket fence and the porch that ran the length of the house, located on the edge of town. He ran up the steps and knocked on the door. When he didn't hear anything at first, he checked his watch and noticed it was only 7:21am. Then the door suddenly opened and the scowl on Al Sokratis' face turned to a smile the moment he saw his only grandson.

Day 5 — November 11, 2019

Chapter 20
The End of the Beginning

Al opened his eyes and was disappointed to find himself in bed alone. The clock on his nightstand read the same time it always did when the alarm was triggered and buzzing. He checked his phone for the date. November 11, 2019. The day he died.

Al showered quickly, or as quickly as one could in their late 70's, and walked down the street to get the papers and a coffee from the store on the corner. He didn't even bother to turn on the television this time. Instead, he waited for what seemed like an interminably long time for the doorbell to ring, checking his watch every few minutes. And just when he had given up all hope that it was going to, it rang.

He leapt from his chair and threw open the front door with surprising force without even bothering to look who was out there. What he found on the other side startled him.

"Hey Sammy boy! Jim?" he said.

"Don't sound so happy to see me, pop," Jimmy laughed, as he let himself in.

"You're out," Al stated.

"Out of where?"

"Umm. Nowhere I guess. What have you been doing with yourself?"

"In the last 12 hours since we went to dinner?"

"Don't you have to work today?"

"I'm the AD. My schedule is flexible."

"You're the AD? Without a degree?"

"Yes. Yes. You were right. I needed to go to school to get my degree. Happy now?"

"Very much so," Al smiled.

"So look, Sammy here has some good news to share."

"Oh yeah? What's that?"

"I asked Delaney to marry me."

"And?"

"And she said YES," Sammy smiled.

"Well, of course she did. She's a smart girl," Al said as he pulled both of them in for a three-way hug.

"I've got a favor to ask," Sammy continued.

"Name it."

"I want you and dad to be my Co-Best Men."

"You worried that neither of us is capable of handling it on our own?" Al laughed.

"Of course not. But it's always been the three of us. The three amigos," Sammy said as he pulled out a picture of them that Al had never seen before. They were dressed in panchos with sombreros and sported fake handlebar mustaches. It must have been taken on Halloween a few years back.

"The three amigos," Al repeated. "When you put it like that, how could I refuse?"

"You can't," Sammy smiled.

"I'm honored. Truly honored. This is without a doubt the greatest honor I've ever received."

"Pop. You received a Purple Heart," Jimmy interjected.

"That was nothing compared to this. You have no idea," Al said, nodding his head as he wiped a tear from his eye.

***

A half hour later, Al pulled up to the local Starbucks. He had driven by it thousands of times, but had never actually been inside it before. The girl behind the counter was pretty and had a great smile. He certainly understood how someone could become infatuated with her.

"I'll have a coffee and a mint hot chocolate with a dollop of whipped cream on top," Al said to her.

"What kind of coffee?" she asked with a smile.

"Umm. Black? Is there another color it comes in?"

"Well, you could get a frappechino or a mochachino or cream and sugar or even pumpkin flavor."

"Just black is fine," Al said.

"No sugar or cream?"

"I'm sweet enough," Al smirked.

"You're cute," she laughed.

And for the briefest of moments, Al thought that maybe he had a shot at getting a bikini picture, but snapped himself out of it in time to see Dennis Devine walk through the door. He was six people back in line when Al paid and grabbed his two coffees.

"Mint hot chocolate with a dollop of whipped cream on top?" Al said, holding out the cup for a man he had never met before.

Dennis didn't know quite how to respond. "How'd you know?"

"I come in here all the time too," Al responded. "Saw you come in and the line looked kind of long, so here you go. Want to join an old man for a few minutes? I'm Al."

No, he really didn't, when he considered the girl that was about ten feet in front of him at the register, but Al had played the age card nicely. "Sure," Dennis said as he sat down. "I'm Dennis."

"So what do you do, Dennis?"

"I'm in sales. How about you?"

"Retired."

"You look really familiar."

"I get that a lot. Generic face."

"You're not Al Sokratis are you? Our former Mayor?"

Al nodded sheepishly. He never knew exactly what the response to that would be.

"Pleasure to meet you. You did a great job. I voted for you. Twice."

"So you're one of the people to blame," Al chuckled. "Married?"

"Yup. Three kids. It's hard work."

"Marriage? Or the kids?"

"Both."

"Well, I'll tell you something that I didn't learn until it was too late. Marriage is hard. So are kids. But they're both extremely rewarding if you take the time to realize it. I lost my wife five years ago now, and I'd give just about anything to get back even one day with her."

"Sounds like you had a great marriage," Dennis remarked.

"Don't get me wrong. We had our peaks and valleys. And sure, there were times I was tempted to stray. I'm sure she was too. Lord knows I'm not the world's best looking guy, nor the easiest to get along with. But then I thought to myself that ten minutes of ice cream wasn't a fair trade for forty years of happiness. If you know what I mean. But listen, I gotta go," Al said as he checked his watch. "It was nice meeting you. Hope to see you again soon."

Fifteen minutes later, a mile down the road, the two men would lock eyes once again, just before everything went black.

Chapter 21
The Reunion

When Al came to, he found himself sitting up in waist high clouds. But there was no Ferrari this time, only Gabriel with an outstretched arm which he used to lift him up.

"Welcome back," Gabriel said.

"You don't seem too surprised to see me," Al answered.

"That's because I'm not."

"Guess I really screwed the pooch."

"I wouldn't say that. But I thought being the best man at your grandson's wedding would be one of your best days."

"It would have been."

"Then why didn't you make sure it happened?"

"Because I found him an even better substitute."

Gabriel nodded. "I understand. Well, you did a lot of things right, my friend. You saved some lives. Personally, I didn't think your little magic trick had a shot in heaven in succeeding," Gabriel laughed, "but it did."

"I didn't know how else to approach it. It was tougher than I thought trying to prevent something from happening without coming across as crazy. But it didn't work out for two of them, plus five people I never met."

"For every decision, there is a ripple effect, and it would have been impossible for you to know what that would have been."

"Still..."

"You also saved your friend's life — twice."

"All I could do was try," Al responded.

"A lot of people try. You actually succeeded."

"Sure. Because I had a second chance. Most people would have success with the benefit of foresight."

"I'm not so sure about that. Most people *could* have success with foresight. But they'd need the right moral compass to follow through with it."

"I guess."

"You even changed the life of someone you didn't know for the better. And gave up one of the best days of your life to do it."

"Life had treated Bill Buckner unfairly. And it was really a two for one deal. Saved my friend and helped out a good man in the process."

"My experience has been that most people use the days for themselves. To re-experience their best days all over again. Occasionally, someone will have a regret they want to fix. But I can't remember the last time someone used their days so unselfishly. Which brings me to the one thing I didn't understand."

"What's that?"

"Why re-live your last day if you weren't going to change it?"

"I tried to.   After you left that night, I watched my last day over and over again trying to find a way to change it for the better. On the 5th time, I noticed a mother and little son driving through the intersection one second before I got hit. If I wasn't there, the guy would have plowed into the woman's car. Probably would have killed them both. So I tried to make Dennis see what he'd be giving up with his flirtation, but then I realized there was nothing I was going to be able to do to stop that. The girl was always going to send the picture whether it was that day or another. And there's no telling what the timing would have been like. So I went for the sure thing. Besides, this was always about one thing for me.   I just couldn't figure out how to do it."

"Maybe you did?" Gabriel smiled.

Al glared at him intensely. "What do you mean?"

"Have a look around," Gabriel said. "Home is always a good place to start."

Gabriel hadn't even finished his sentence before Al was off running through the clouds. He was tearing through them like he was racing for the end zone in high school. He felt as free and energetic as a teenager, as if he could run all day, with an excitement the likes of which you only felt once or twice in your entire lifetime. Gradually, the clouds dissipated into a beautiful, warm, sunny summer day, revealing a small town street with perfectly manicured lawns and gardens. He was in his old neighborhood, the recognition of which caused him to pick up even more speed as he raced past the houses of all their friends, before halting to a stop at the house on the corner with the white picket fence — his house.

Al leapt up the front steps two at a time and threw open the screen door in such a rush that he nearly pulled it off its hinges. He ran through the living room and stopped cold in the entry way to the kitchen.

"Brooklyn," he said softly.

"Brooklyn is a borough of New York City. My name is Brooke," she answered with her sweet smile.

"Not anymore it isn't."

She looked the same age as she had been the day he first met her and was wearing the same yellow, floral print dress, that was light and flowing to just above mid-thigh. He caught a sideways glance at the mirror in the living room and noticed that he was now twenty-seven as well, handsome and chiseled with a sly grin that women had always found irresistible.

"I wasn't expecting you so soon," she said.

"What can I say? I missed you too much to wait any longer."

She jumped into his arms and wrapped her legs tightly around his waist as if she never planned on letting go again. He kissed her, softly and gently, the way he had the very first time. And he knew at that moment, he was experiencing his very best day.

Author Notes

I have to admit I was hesitant to write this book. Any time you have some measure of success with an original story, writing a sequel to it seems daunting. Could it possibly live up to the original? Not that the original *Five Days* was *War and Peace*, *The Great Gatsby* or *The Catcher in the Rye* in terms of influence on the American literary world. But it did have its share of loyal fans that I didn't want to disappoint.

In the end, I decided that I would only write the follow up as a stand alone book—meaning the idea remained the same, but the characters and story were all new. And only, if I thought I could create a character as compelling and interesting as the Mike Postman character in the original. Whether I did or not is obviously up to you to decide. What I love about this series is that it enables me to take trips down memory lane, incorporating people and days from my own life, while also sending me on a journey through days in history that I'd previously only read about or seen clips of on television.

I hope that you enjoyed the trip as well while thinking about which days you would choose, or which days from history you would change if you could…Be well.

MM

Enjoy this book?   Turn the page for a preview of the original story that started it all-- FIVE DAYS...

FIVE DAYS

I
~THE END OF THE BEGINNING~

The warmth and sun-drenched days of late summer, had been replaced by the cold, darkness of November, where the crisp chill served as a precursor to a winter that would long overstay its welcome once the holidays had past. Students that were eager to learn something new and different back in August had been replaced by unmotivated, and occasionally cruel creatures that were recognizable as human beings only by their DNA.

When the bell sounded signaling the end of another particularly draining day, it was difficult to determine who was happier—the students or the teachers. Mike Postman flipped the Algebra textbook he had been teaching from closed, waved as the students poured from the room, and sat at his desk for the obligatory twenty minutes mandated by the teachers' contract.

Mike looked like he was in his early 30's, but was actually nearly 40, with the sort of generic good looks that enabled him to pass as either the clean-cut boy next door, or a Hollywood character actor. He pulled into the driveway of his modest two-story cottage across the street from one of the oldest beaches in Southwestern Connecticut. On this day, he didn't even go inside, but instead, immediately crossed to where the multi-million dollar homes stood. It wasn't much of a stretch to say that his home could have passed as a guesthouse for any one of them.

Walking on the path that ran along the Connecticut shoreline, Mike bit down his lower lip, the way he frequently did anytime he was thinking. Autumn always had a certain smell to it, he thought; even back when he was a kid. Not a strong one, mind you, but rather a soft, subtle smell, not unlike the gentle scent of a woman's perfume as she walked past. The interesting thing was that autumn smelled differently depending on where you were. In Florence, Italy, autumn was damp and musty, clinging to your senses like a memory you would never forget. In Chicago, autumn smelled like burning leaves. In New York City, it smelled like roasted chestnuts and Italian sausage. And in Woodmont - on - the - Sound, Connecticut, the smell of autumn was crisp and clean, like a freshly laundered shirt.

Gone were the roller bladers and sun bathers of summer. Weather wise, this day was symbolic of his mood; colder than it looked, with clouds battling the blue sky for prominence. As a profession, teaching was simultaneously rewarding and frustrating. On more than one occasion, he had thought about trying something different, but he didn't know what else he was suited to do. Besides, the highs of teaching were generally higher than anything else he could imagine doing. There was nothing quite like seeing the smile of a struggling teenager after you had managed to give them some measure of hope. And yet, for every time he felt as though he was making a difference, something would happen as if to not so gently remind him that just maybe he was wrong about that.

He heard the faint shout of a little boy as he came around the bend. Barely audible at first, he was so entrenched in thought, he didn't even notice at first. But it grew louder with each successive shout, as a boy of about ten approached him frantically.

"Mister! Mister! My friend just fell in off the pier and he can't swim! I'm not good enough to pull him out! Please help!"

Mike didn't hesitate, throwing his jacket onto the ground and kicking off his shoes as he ran to the end of the pier and dove in headfirst. It was abundantly clear that he wasn't a strong swimmer himself, but after a few awkward strokes, he managed to reach the boy.

Holding him around his neck with his right hand gripping the boy's shirt collar, he dragged him along, struggling to keep himself above water in the process. With the other boy lying prone on the pier with an outstretched arm, Mike swung around and tried throwing the boy toward the arm.   Once he saw that the boy's friend had grabbed him and helped lift him onto the pier, Mike relaxed, and then suddenly, and yet almost peacefully, plunged beneath the surface of the water.   For the briefest of moments, he felt himself taking in water-- through his nose, mouth, and ears. His eyes were burning from the salt water. His lungs felt as though they were about to explode. And then he felt *nothing* at all.

When he came to, he found himself lying amongst a bevy of soft, white, puffy, cumulus clouds. He staggered to his feet just in time to see a tram, not unlike one you might find at Disney World, approaching in the far off distance. It seemed to make up several miles in a few moments, before it eased to a stop directly in front of him.

"Let's go, Mike. Get on," the driver said impatiently.

"Where are you going?" he asked.

"You'll know when you get there," was the

response.

How did he know him? Where was he? And why was he the youngest one on board by at least 25 years?

The tram tunneled through the clouds, emerging at the front gate of what appeared to be Caesar's Palace. Not the one from ancient Rome, but rather the one that had been modeled after it on the Las Vegas strip.

"This is your stop," the driver said, matter-of-factly, a nod of his head indicating he was supposed to get off.

When no one else moved toward the exit, Mike realized the man was talking to him, and he stepped off the tram.

"How did I end up in Vegas?" he asked no one in particular.

The response came from a voice behind him.

"You didn't," the voice said.

It was a deep, James Earl Jones-like voice.

"I didn't?"

"No. But we had to do something. We were getting too many complaints that our accommodations weren't as nice as those down below. His home looks like Graceland."

The man was African-American, wearing a white, flowing gown that was a cross between a priest's robe and a Roman toga.

"Elvis lives downstairs?" Mike asked in a perpetual state of disbelief and confusion.

"Of course not," the man laughed. "Elvis is a music teacher in Wisconsin."

Mike nodded as if this somehow made sense. "Then who's down below?" he asked.

"Beelzebub. Satan. You probably know him more readily as the devil."

"So if he's downstairs, then that must mean I'm in…"

The man nodded. "Gabriel--at your service."

"How did I end up here, Gabriel?"

"You died saving that little boy's life. Or should I say—you *let* yourself die."

"I don't really recall that much about it," Mike responded, "And I don't mean that in a Bill Clintonesque sort of way."

"Your memory will come back a little at a time as you need it," Gabriel assured him.

Mike glanced around him and nodded at an elderly couple that walked past. They didn't even acknowledge him.

"If this is heaven, Gabriel, how come no one's very friendly?"

"Oh, they're not going to be friendly to you, Mike."

"Why not?" he asked, offended.

Gabriel stopped walking—took on a more serious tone now. "Because you took your own life, while most of these people has theirs taken away from them."

He decided not to waste too much time thinking about it. He simply had too many questions that needed to be answered.

"Then why am I here, if I'm such a bad guy?"

"Did I say you were a bad guy?"

"You implied as much."

"Don't read too much into things," Gabriel answered, his tone much more cordial once again. "And you're here because you're visiting."

"I'm visiting?"

Mike didn't much care for the sound of that.

"Is this some sort of a tryout?" he followed up with.

Mike had always hated tryouts. It didn't matter whether it was an athletic team, the school play, or a job interview. He wanted to be wanted. He didn't want to have to convince someone he was good enough.

"Of course not."

"So after I visit, then what?"

"Then you go back."

"Then I go back," Mike repeated.

"Do you always repeat everything people say to you?" Gabriel asked.

"Only when I think they're full of..."

He stopped himself just short of finishing his sentence. He thought better of it considering his surroundings, and also how tenuous his tenure there appeared to be.

"So I get to go back where?" he continued.

"To where you came from. To any year you like actually. You've been given a great gift, Mike. You've been given the opportunity to go back and relive any five days from your life of your own choosing."

"And why exactly do I get to do that?"

"Have you ever wished you had the chance to do something over? To go back knowing then what you know now?"

"Of course. Doesn't everyone?"

"Well, you have the opportunity to do that."

"Does everyone get to go back?"

"Not everyone," Gabriel answered cryptically.

"Then why me?"

"It will all be explained to you in time. But we really need to get going."

With that, Gabriel smiled a knowing smile and held the casino door open for him to enter. Mike bit down on his lower lip as they walked past the cavalcade of high-end shops just inside the entrance, while the distant chiming of slot machines and occasional screams of joy echoed down the corridor.

"So, Gabriel," Mike said with a wink, "do they have any ten dollar craps tables at this time of day?"

"We don't use money to gamble up here."

"Then what do you use? Cars? Clothes? Women?" He winked again, and made a clicking sound with his tongue.

"People gamble for the thrill of beating the system," he answered simply.

"Don't you think it would add an additional thrill if a cool grand was riding on one toss of the dice?"

"It wouldn't matter. People have no use for money here. Everything is already provided for them.   Food,   clothing,   shelter, entertainment, transportation…"

"Sounds like a communist block nation. Well, if they don't need money, what would be the incentive to work?"

"Most people don't.   Most people have worked their entire lives and are glad not to have to any longer."

"But then how does anything get done?"

He rethought his question as soon as the words left his mouth. After all, it was heaven.

"Some people choose to work anyway."

"Why would anyone *choose* to work?" Mike asked. It was a concept he had a difficult time wrapping his arms around. Most days, he had come home so exhausted both mentally and physically, that he wasn't sure he would be able to do it again 12 hours later. Of course he always had, but if anyone had given him a choice, he would have gladly chosen to follow the Mets around the country instead.

"You yourself once said that if you won the lottery, you would still work, only without having to worry about money, you'd take a job where you really felt as though you could make a difference."

"How do you know I said that?" Mike asked. It was true. He had said it. But he was trying to impress a girl at the time and thought it sounded better than drinking beer, following the Mets and playing Xbox.

"I know everything there is to know about you,

Mike. Except for one thing."

"And what's that?"

"All in good time, my friend," Gabriel said as they continued down the narrowing corridor.